"An adventure in the Alaskan wilderness with smoke jumping wildfire firefighters. This Christian suspense will give you all the feels with the family dynamic between the firefighters and the push and pull between Tori and Orion, all while keeping you on the edge of your seat with the suspense wondering what is going to come next. Once you pick it up, you won't want to put it down until you have finished it!"

—Laramee, GOODREADS

"Awesome book from beginning to end! I truly enjoy reading anything Michelle writes and this book was no exception. Loved reading Orion and Tori's story as they navigate the wilds of Alaska and a fake marriage to get back to base and the rest of their crew. Can't wait for the next one!"

—Kate, GOODREADS

"This was another thrilling installment in this Christian Romantic Suspense series. Taking off where book 1 left off, we follow Orion and Tori as they have an adventure full of injuries and a journey towards faith. This book has a large amount of suspense as we are strung along on the series wide mystery. I love the Alaskan wilderness setting. This was a great read and I can't wait until the next one is available!"

—**Michaela, Goodreads**

BURNING ESCAPE

CHASING FIRE ALASKA | BOOK 3

BURNING ESCAPE

MICHELLE SASS ALECKSON

sunrise
PUBLISHING

Burning Escape
Chasing Fire: Alaska, Book 3

Copyright © 2025 Sunrise Media Group LLC
Print ISBN: 978-1-963372-98-4

This book is a work of fiction. Names, characters, places, and incidents are
either products of the author's imagination or used fictitiously. Any simi-
larity to actual people, organizations, and/or events is purely coincidental.
All Scripture quotations, unless otherwise indicated, are taken from the
The ESV® Bible (The Holy Bible, English Standard Version®), © 2001
by Crossway, a publishing ministry of Good News Publishers. Used by
permission. All rights reserved.

For more information about Michelle Sass Aleckson please access the
author's website at www.michellealeckson.com.

Published in the United States of America.

Cover Design: Sunrise Media Group LLC

· CHASING FIRE ALASKA ·

To those who long for home,
a place to belong.
May you know the love God has for you
and find the shelter in the shadow
of His wings.

Blessed be the Lord, who daily bears our burden,
the God who is our salvation.
Our God is a God who saves; from the Sovereign
Lord comes escape from death.

PSALM 68:19-20NIV

Eight weeks earlier

HE'D MADE IT. AFTER YEARS OF dreaming, all the training, and months of planning, Orion Price was finally ready for his shot at fulfilling the heroic legacy of Grandpa Jack.

Alaska was definitely cooler than Ember, Montana. A different ridgeline loomed in the distance rather than the mountains of the Kootenai National Forest Orion knew by heart, having grown up in their shadow. Here, Denali's peak soared above the neighboring summits. Impressive, no doubt. A little intimidating . . . but mostly it sparked excitement for the adventure ahead. The adventure he'd been waiting for since he was a kid.

Orion stepped into the Midnight Sun Saloon, the smell of meat, smoky and spicy, making his mouth water. Usually a day of traveling—flying from Bozeman to Seattle to Anchorage, plus the two-hour drive to Copper Mountain—would make for a long day, but the way adrenaline was surging through him, he was ready for a good meal and to let off a little steam. He had something to celebrate.

He must not be the only one. Live music from a band out on the patio traipsed in on the breeze through an open window.

Orion found a seat next to Logan Crawford at the bar. The woman serving took his order for wings and a beer without fuss or chitchat. Within moments, a tall lager in an iced glass was plopped down in front of him. He took a long, slow sip, savoring the cold drink.

He'd put in his time with the Jude County hotshot team. He was ready for smokejumping. He just had to get through the training and nab one of the open rookie spots. He glanced at Logan next to him. His buddy from Montana had snagged an open spot on the team already, showing up at the last minute before the season began. He'd been a smokejumper in Ember and had even done a stint fighting bushfires in Australia. While Orion had grown up at Wildlands

Academy learning all about fighting wildfires, he was still pretty young.

But he knew what he wanted, and he would do whatever it took. His mom—his only family for most of his life—was finally settled and now had Charlie and Orion's new half sister Alexis nearby. It gave him the freedom to spread his wings now, knowing she was happy and fulfilled.

This was his time. Finally.

A loud cry rose from the rowdy group at the other end of the bar as the bunch of bearded men downed shots. They were dirty, a little scruffy, and looked like they'd stumbled out of the wilds for a good time and didn't care much who they disturbed with their ruckus. The tall guy in the middle of the pack threw back another shot and howled at the ceiling while his buddies laughed and slapped him on the back.

"Hey, pipe down, boys. Some of us want to hear the music," the bartender yelled over her shoulder.

"Sure thing, Vic," one of the guys said with a fake smile. Then he turned back to the group and rolled his eyes.

Logan chatted with a couple of women sitting on the other side of him. Orion had never been great at flirting. Might as well let Logan charm the ladies. Instead, Orion turned on his stool to take in the view of the mountains.

His eye caught a petite blonde woman walking toward one of the high-top tables and the two girls waving to her. As she skirted around another party, a guy in a hockey jersey was pushing away from his table.

Right into the woman's path.

Orion jumped off his seat in time to catch her as her foot caught on the chair. She grabbed his arms before she could hit the ground.

She blew a strand of long blonde hair out of her face, and he caught her wide-eyed gaze.

Wow.

Talk about Alaskan beauty. She didn't have that fake look of a lot of makeup. Just a clean glow, a smattering of freckles across her dainty nose, and wide blue eyes that reminded him of a deep mountain lake. Fathomless and gorgeous.

Her surprise quickly melted into a dazzling grin.

"You all right, ma'am?" he asked her, helping set her back on her feet.

"Ma'am? How old do you think I am?" She gave him a mock glare and then chuckled as she dusted off her jeans.

Heat rushed to his neck and cheeks. Oh, he was so bad at this. But she didn't let go of his arm.

And he was totally okay with that.

He grimaced. "Sorry. Where I'm from, it's a sign of respect."

"And where's that?" A flirty lilt in her voice drew him in. "You're too polite to be from around here."

Maybe he should be thanking the guy who'd tripped her.

He cleared his throat. "I'm from Montana."

"Ry, food's here!" Logan called from behind him. Right. Food. His job. This wasn't the time for distractions.

"I'd better go." He nodded to Logan and turned back to the gorgeous woman. "Don't want him to steal my dinner."

"Can't have that." She chuckled. "Thanks for the save, Montana."

He tipped his chin. "Anytime."

Well, okay then. Nothing quite said "Welcome to Alaska!" like a beautiful woman falling into his arms.

He could get used to this life.

Orion found his seat and dug into the steaming hot food waiting at his spot. His wings were spicy and sweet, the fries salty and crisp, just the way he liked them. See, this was what he'd been waiting for. Food even tasted better in Alaska. Adventure was in the air, and tomorrow he'd start his new job. His new life.

Logan didn't say much as they ate. Orion enjoyed his beer and scanned the crowd. Okay, so yes, he was hoping to catch another glimpse of the blonde elfin creature with big blue eyes that had fallen into his arms. The floral, almost woodsy scent she'd carried still stuck with him. Must be the excitement of finally stepping into his legacy. It wasn't like he believed in love at first sight or anything like it.

"Wanna get some fresh air? It's getting a little warm in here." Logan stood and dropped cash on the bar top.

"Sure."

With a full belly and half a beer still left to enjoy, Orion followed Logan to the deck outside. Some of the crowd were using the space to dance to the country-rock band. A flash of blonde hair, and Orion found what he'd been looking for.

The woodland sprite threw her head back and laughed as she twirled to the music. Her hands clapped high above her head as she swayed her hips. A few other girls joined her, each with a drink in their hands. But their eyes were clear, no one acted tipsy. Just a bunch of friends out for a good time.

"Why don't you go join them?" Logan bumped his shoulder. "You know you want to."

Why? Because he'd never been the Casanova type. And he'd grown up in the wilderness. Literally.

But after working an intense fire season together last year, he and Logan knew each other pretty well. Orion didn't feel the need to keep up pretenses—especially with a fellow believer who might be his roommate for the summer. "I wouldn't know the first thing about how to do that. And I have no clue how to dance."

"That's all that's stopping you? Dude, you fight wildfires. This is easy. You go out, ask the woman to dance, and feel the beat. Figure out the rest as you go."

Orion watched them another moment. The sun glinted off the woman's blonde hair as she spun. She was the picture of light and beauty and freedom.

"Go, Tia!" one of her friends called as she gave her a high five.

Tia.

The name fit. Confident and cute and . . .

My goodness, he'd just met the woman. What was wrong with him?

Okay, yes, he wanted to dance with her.

"If it's so easy, why aren't you out there?" He glanced at Logan.

His smirk dimmed. "That's not why I'm here."

"Why *are* you here? All winter, you never said anything when I brought up the fact that I was moving here. Then you call me up out of the blue and tell me you're joining too."

"I didn't know then."

"Know what?"

"That she was coming here." Logan finished the last bit of his drink.

"So there's a woman involved."

"Isn't there always?" Logan looked out past the patio lights at the mountains guarding the town, his usually jolly mood suddenly somber.

"What's her name?"

"Jamie Winters." He turned to Orion. "If you like this woman, ask her to dance. Don't let the moment pass by. You might not get another chance." He clapped him on the shoulder as he stood. "I'm going back to the hotel. Training starts at zero six hundred."

But with the Alaska sun still high in the sky,

no hint of setting just yet, Orion was reluctant to join him. "I'll just finish my beer."

Logan gave him a knowing nod and left.

After one more song and finishing his own drink, Orion still debated. Really, he should leave. He didn't need any distractions. Not now that his goal was within reach. He stood. One more glimpse couldn't hurt though.

There she was. Still dancing. But her friends were gone.

And the rowdy group of guys from the bar swooped in.

The big guy in woodsy camouflage, their leader, wrapped a beefy arm around the woman. "A little thing like you shouldn't be alone on the dance floor."

She swatted his arm away. "Get lost. I'm not alone."

"Sure looks like it." He moved in again. The woman pulled away, but one of the camo pack snuck behind and blocked her in.

That was it.

Orion jogged over. "Hey, honey, sorry I'm late." He flashed a big grin and held out his hand, wanting to give her a choice.

She hesitated a moment. Looked him in the

eye, almost as if she was trying to discern his wor-
thiness as a rescuer.

A second later, a bright smile lit the whole
dance floor, and her warm hand was in his.

"It's about time, Montana. I've been waiting
all night."

Tori Mitchell had one night of freedom and
letting loose before another intense summer, and
she was going to make the most of every second
of it.

This was her year. She was going to make that
smokejumper team no matter what. And chances
were good. She was in the best shape of her life.
She'd trained all winter. Sacrificed so much.

So for this one evening, she'd forget about the
strict discipline she used to keep everything in
order and instead enjoy herself, having finally ac-
cepted the invite to go out to the Midnight Sun
Saloon. She'd listen to the band play and let the
music move her instead of holding back like she
usually did.

And she certainly wouldn't let some jerk on
the dance floor ruin her night.

"Hey, honey, sorry I'm late." Montana, the
handsome stranger in the navy shirt and flannel,

held out a hand to her. His blue-eyed gaze locked in on her. He'd caught her earlier, blushed when she'd teased him about calling her ma'am. He had a nice Captain America vibe going on—if the Cap had come from the wilds of Montana instead of NYC.

Her hero could totally take Camo Man on with those wide shoulders, but he was trying to defuse the situation and rescue her.

She could take care of herself. But maybe for this one time it would be okay. She didn't want to fill out a police report on her one night off.

"It's about time, Montana. I've been waiting all night." She gave him her warmest smile and was finally able to pull away, since Camo released his hold on her arm.

Even if his foul breath hadn't been enough to warn her, she'd made enough mistakes with men to steer clear of someone like him.

Montana, on the other hand, was probably too good for the likes of her. He followed her lead to the other side of the dance floor. The music slowed.

He bent down. "I think the coast is clear. You don't really have to dance with me. I only wanted to help."

Yup. He was definitely out of her league.

But her mouth didn't know better.

"I came here to enjoy the music tonight." So what harm could it do to dance a little under the stars? Especially with a cute guy with dark hair falling in wild waves across his forehead. A guy who blushed.

Besides, he was probably another tourist passing through who she'd never see again.

"So maybe you could help me out?" she asked him.

"Of course. How?" He looked so sincere.

"Like this." She faced him and lightly looped her arms around his shoulders. They were nice shoulders. He wasn't big and bulky, but he was definitely fit, maybe worked out, the way his biceps bulged in the dark-blue T-shirt and flannel he wore.

He cleared his throat and dropped his head, spoke in her ear. "I, uh, I . . . don't really know how to dance."

How refreshing to find a guy who could admit he *couldn't* do something. His eyes were honest and true. And that slight flush to his cheeks only made the blue-green flecks stand out.

"That's all right. Just follow my lead." She placed his hands on her hips, where his light touch warmed her through.

"Yes, ma'am." He swallowed, looked her in the eye, and gave her a bit of a shy smile.

Oh, she could fall for this one. Sweet and polite. And he did, in fact, follow her lead as they swayed to the crooning from the stage with a soulful fiddle accompaniment. The kind of song made for luring people to fall in love.

But it was only for tonight. So no danger of that.

She moved a little closer to him, the solidness and heat drawing her in, a hint of amber and sandalwood wrapping her in a sweet embrace. "You're doing great, Montana. Who said you can't dance?"

"No one. I haven't done it before."

"Shall we take it up a notch?"

His eyebrow quirked up in a question. "Are you flirting with me?"

She chuckled. His honest question and lack of guile was refreshing. "Wow, you really don't get out much, do you?"

He sucked in a breath through his teeth. "That obvious, huh?"

"Here. Hold tight to my hand. I'm gonna spin out, and then you lightly pull me back in. Nothing to it."

"I think I can handle that."

And he did. She twirled out, her hair dancing on the cool breeze with his strong grip anchoring her. A slight tug and she spun back into his arms, rested her hand on his chest, her fingers hitting his well-defined pectorals.

He definitely worked out.

"That wasn't so hard, was it?" she asked.

A slow, lazy grin emerged on his face. "Not at all."

They danced to the next slow song, Tori tucking herself against him. The crisp spring breezes swirled through the crowd but didn't cool the air between them. The song drew to a close, the last notes floating away into the soft light of Alaskan twilight. The lead singer announced the band was going to take a little break before coming back.

"Could I . . . buy you a drink? Or a meal if you like?" He looked at her directly, a hint of vulnerability there. Not weakness by any means, but a hope that—dang—she wanted to realize for him. Looking around, she saw her friends Evie and Lucy talking with a couple of guys they knew.

Well, she *was* hungry. And it was her *one* night, so, "Sure, but why don't we get a snack to go. There's a great park by the river where we can eat." And with plenty of tourists out and about, she didn't have to worry about being too secluded.

She was rewarded with a handsome smile. They put in a to-go order for ribs and onion rings.

While waiting for their food, someone tapped Tori on the shoulder. She turned to find one of her regulars from work.

"Hey, Damian." He looked different in jeans and a fitted shirt that showed off all his hard work at the gym. Tall and lean with dark-blond hair cut short and stylish, he had a cute brunette on his arm.

"Hey, Tori. This is my friend Amber. I was just telling her what a great trainer you are and that she should ask for you at the gym."

"Aw, that's sweet. I'm going to be gone for the summer though. But for sure come see me this fall when I'm back."

"I'll do that." Amber smiled. Damian started to ask something else, but Montana was paying for their food. Tori quickly said goodbye and turned back to the bar.

"I can pay for that." Tori started to pull out her debit card from her jeans pocket.

"No need. It's already done." His clear, steady gaze quieted the accusations and doubts. Maybe letting someone take care of her for a night wasn't so bad. As long as she didn't get used to it.

Once their food was ready, they strolled out

along the main drag and headed to the riverside park.

"So, what do you do around here for work?" he asked. "Or are you on vacation?"

"I live here. But let's not talk about work. I've given myself this one night to forget about jobs and responsibilities. That's for tomorrow."

"So you're one of those live-in-the-moment kind of people?"

"Tonight I am."

He chuckled. "Fair enough. So what do I call you? At least for tonight. I thought I heard someone call you Tia?"

"I'm—" For tonight, she wanted to be someone different. Someone without her past, without the bad choices weighing her down. At least with this man, who had honor written all over him, from the way he'd rescued her on the dance floor to the fact that he'd paid for her meal. "—Victoria." She held out her hand. He shook it.

"Nice to meet you, Victoria." His hand was calloused, the shake firm, but he didn't squeeze like he had something to prove.

Wouldn't that be nice?

He didn't let go right away. "I'm Orion."

"You're named after the Greek hunter?"

"The constellation."

"Ah, so you're a star."

"Nah, just an ordinary guy from Montana with a weird name. What about you? Are you from Alaska?"

"California."

"So what brought you up here?"

"Regrets. A man. Take your pick." She grabbed an onion ring and ripped it in half, popped a piece in her mouth. Shoot. Why had she said that? She sent him a playful wink to dispel any sense of pity that he might throw her way.

"But the joke's on him. I found a career I love. A good group of friends. I stayed, and he's gone, so . . ." She shrugged as she ate the rest of the o-ring. "So for now, Alaska is the closest thing I have to a home."

Maybe someday she'd find a place where she belonged. Her sisters kept asking when she'd settle down and find a permanent address. But like they could talk. They had both moved multiple times in the last couple years, even though now they both claimed Last Chance County was home sweet home for them.

She wiped her fingers on a napkin. "What about you? What brings you here?"

"An opportunity. I love Montana, but I wanted a chance for something bigger in a place I didn't have a history or connections. I want to be able to say I did this on my own, ya know?"

"I do. I have two older sisters that are ... amazing, but also a lot. They practically raised me, so I kinda get it, but they are always checking on me like they don't believe I can handle myself, even though I'm grown up and have been on my own for years. So, yeah, I can respect the need to be your own person, even if it means starting from scratch."

"Exactly." His blue eyes lit with understanding ... connection.

They enjoyed the rest of their ribs and onion rings, chatted about useless things, and listened to the frogs along the river. Tourists wandered past. The sun drifted toward the horizon.

A text notification dinged from Tori's phone. The time glared up at her from the screen. "Shoot. It's almost midnight! I should get back."

"Afraid your carriage will turn back to a pumpkin?" Orion stood to throw the to-go boxes away.

"No, I just have an early morning." A morning she needed to be at her best for. She'd worked too hard for that smokejumper spot to flounder now. "I set my alarm for midnight. I have to head back."

"I'll walk with you." Orion's dark hair, longer on top, ruffled in the wind, which had picked up.

"Here." He shook off his flannel and laid it over her shoulders.

She wrapped herself up in its warmth and amber scent. She really shouldn't let herself enjoy this.

But it wasn't midnight yet.

They walked toward the saloon, a faster pace than they'd set on the way out. At one point, their hands brushed, and their fingers tangled up together. She didn't pull away. His slow smile, that slight blush, was still visible under the streetlights, and the glow of the almost full moon sent a thrill through her.

Sheesh. She was like a teenager all over again. If only she'd waited back then for a man like Orion.

They reached the edge of the parking lot at the Midnight Sun Saloon, the band music still going strong though the parking lot wasn't as full as earlier. They stopped by the road sign.

"I had a really nice night, Victoria." He still held her hand. "Would you—" He glanced down a second and then back to her eyes, a question there she didn't want to answer the way she needed to.

So she kissed him.

A sweet, simple kiss, lightly pressing her lips to his. But it heated her clear down to her toes.

Her smartwatch buzzed, killing the moment. Midnight.

She pulled back, untangled herself from him. "This was . . . amazing, but I'm sorry. I have to go." Her night of freedom was over.

"Can I see you again?"

Oh, this was harder than she'd thought. She swallowed down a thickness in her throat. "I'm sorry, Orion, but that won't work. I only had tonight. I have to leave, and I'll be gone for quite a while."

"I'm a patient guy."

Of course he was. "No, Orion." Why were her eyes stinging? She'd just met him. And yes, he was gentlemanly and kind, but she couldn't afford any distractions.

And let's be honest, when it came to men, she had horrible luck.

"I'm leaving. I've got . . . important work to do."

"I get that, but what does that have to do with—"

"Let's just end on a good note, huh?" She grazed her fingers along his jaw and planted one last kiss on his cheek. Looking down, she caught the glint of something on his neck. A cross.

Well, that was a deal breaker right there. Good thing she was already leaving.

She turned and walked away. Didn't turn back. Didn't look.

A part of her wanted to, but there were more important things in life. Tomorrow, she would be fighting for one of the smokejumper spots, and she couldn't let anything get in her way.

Eventually, she heard Orion's footsteps in the gravel, heading away. He wasn't following her.

Good. That was what she wanted.

She reached her little Honda Civic sitting on the other side of the lot. The parking lot light overhead glinted off a spiderweb of cracks on the windshield.

Tori whipped around, scanning the area for anyone lurking in the shadows. Who had done this?

A small piece of paper fluttered under her wiper blade.

You can't escape this time.

Orion rushed down the stairs to the lobby, too late and impatient to wait for the elevator. Today was the first step to living out his dream and doing what he was born to do.

"Dude, come on!" Logan shoved a hotel coffee

into Orion's hand. "Don't wanna be late for your first day of training."

Right. Orion tried to shake off the memory of the mysterious and captivating Victoria from last night. A memory that tangled up in his head way more than he liked.

"You okay? You look awful." Logan glanced over from behind the wheel of his car.

He wasn't thrilled to have Logan following him to the Midnight Sun crew, but the guy had his own reasons for coming up here, and maybe it wouldn't be horrible to have a friend around. As long as Orion was seen as his own person.

"I'm fine. Didn't sleep great."

"Nervous?"

Sure, let Logan think that was it. "Maybe."

"You got back pretty late last night, but you're a good firefighter, Price. You've got this."

"Thanks."

Orion sipped his coffee. Ugh. Lukewarm.

So different from Victoria. She was fire and heat. And boy, had he been burned all right.

What was his problem anyway? It had been one dance. One kiss.

But it had hooked him like an expert fisherman catching a king salmon, snagging on his heart and pulling relentlessly. No other woman had done that before.

But what did it say that she'd felt no qualms about kissing him and leaving? Obviously the moment hadn't unraveled her as it had him. Maybe her job really *was* important. Or he'd simply been a distraction for her.

Whatever.

He needed his head on straight. This was his time to show everyone that he had what it took. He'd left his home, his family, everything he knew in Ember for this. He was ready to step into his legacy. And maybe redeem himself, at least a little.

They pulled into the base camp. Quonset huts, a few log-sided cabins, and a long building labeled as a mess hall all surrounded the small runway crossing through the middle of the camp. A couple of helipads and a small lot of RVs sat off to the side. The base was tucked up against foothills, out in the middle of nowhere. The crisp morning air smelled like new beginnings. Orion and Logan parked and walked into one of the open plane hangars. People milled around chatting. A small group off to the side of the room caught his eye. What in the world—

"Hey, the Trouble Boys and Sanchez are here?" Orion asked Logan.

"Guess so." Logan walked up and gave a fist bump to Hammer. "What are you guys doing here? Get too hot in Montana?"

"Something like that." Hammer grinned. "We've been here all winter. I thought you were staying with Jude County."

"Plans changed." Logan pointed his thumb at Orion. "Thought I'd keep an eye on the rookie here. Thinks he wants to jump out of planes this year."

Orion clenched his jaw tight.

Funny. Logan didn't bring up the fact that he was here because of a woman named Jamie Winters with *these* guys. It was bad enough he thought he needed to watch over Orion. Now more of the Jude County crew were here? Who else had come up from Montana for the summer?

This was supposed to be his fresh start, a chance to work with people that didn't know him. He was supposed to do this on his own.

"You wanna be a smokejumper?" Kane asked Orion. "Between the locals and the smokejumpers from Montana, I heard there aren't many spots. We'll be joining the hotshots." The look on his face said he wouldn't have minded trying out but something had stopped him.

"Guess we'll see who gets them." Because Orion

was going to nab one of the open spots no matter what. He had to. After all he'd gone through to get his mother on board with this career—which had been no easy feat, since her own father had lost his life smokejumping—he wasn't going to turn back now. At least he wasn't competing with Kane, Hammer, and the others.

A sharp whistle stopped all conversation. Everyone turned to the front of the room, where a man with a clipboard and—wait. Was that Jade Ransom? Another Jude County transplant. Seriously, had the whole crew decided to follow him here?

"I'm Tucker Newman. I'm the commander this season. This is Jade Ransom. She's jump boss, and she's running the show if you're here to train for smokejumping. If that's you, head out with her. The rest of you stick here with Mitch Bronson, who will be running the hotshot crew."

Orion and Logan and about fifteen others followed Jade out to a bay garage, doors wide open, letting the cool morning breeze in.

"Orion, good to see you." JoJo Butcher walked over to them. She ruffled Orion's hair. "You're not gonna get your pretty hair messed up jumping out of planes, are ya?"

Like he needed one more person here treating

him like a little kid when he was trying to prove he was his own man. He swatted her hand away. "What are you doing here?"

"Jade is from here originally. She said she was moving back and asked if I wanted to come. Sounded like fun, so I decided to join her."

Great.

Logan gave her a fist bump. "Good to see you."

Jade faced the group. "I'm not much of one for talking this early, so I hope you came ready to work. At the end of our training, two of you will be given a spot on my crew. Most of you have done this before, but for you newbies, this is no walk in the park. It's brutal because you are going into one of the most dangerous situations a person can face. I will push you to your limits because wildland fires don't care. Now, drop your stuff, grab one of the packs along this wall, and get ready to run."

"Good luck, newbie." Logan smirked as he grabbed one of the packs.

Orion didn't need luck though. He was born for this, so the joke was on Logan. As they lined up, Jade checked people off on the clipboard. When she got to the end of the line, she looked around. "Anyone seen Mitchell?"

After a chorus of *no*s and heads shaking, Jade

blew out a short breath and made a mark on the clipboard.

Tough break, Mitchell—whoever that was. But it was one less person vying for a place on the team. Orion smiled.

Just as they were about to start, a dusty Honda Civic with a broken windshield screeched as it swung into the parking lot.

"Wait!" a woman cried as she jumped out of the car.

Jade went out to meet her. What little Orion could see of the newcomer was weirdly familiar. But a baseball cap covered her hair, and the sunglasses she wore and Jade's shadow obscured her features.

"Must be Mitchell," Logan said. "Not a great way to make a first impression. Jade hates when people are late."

All the better for Orion.

Jade turned back to the line. "Let's go!" she yelled over her shoulder. "Mitchell, you have some catching up to do."

As Jade stepped away, slanted sunlight hit the woman, brightening her features. Blonde hair streamed behind "Mitchell's" ball cap.

Orion's smile dimmed. A force like a fist dropped into his gut.

What in the world was Victoria doing here?

"Dude, come on!" Logan nudged Orion's shoulder. The rest of the line was already running. Orion gave himself a shake and followed Logan. He glanced back and saw Victoria rushing to heft one of the heavy packs onto her back. By the time they reached the road, she had caught up to them, though she was huffing pretty hard.

"Important work, huh?" Orion tried to take the bite out of his words, but she'd blown him off last night. Made it sound like she was leaving town or something. And now they had to compete for one of the few smokejumper spots?

Her eyes widened. "Orion?" Victoria's face was already flushed, and his name sounded more like a wheezy breath as they jogged up the inclined road with their packs. After a pause, she spoke again. "Well," she said as she huffed, "it *is* an important job. I didn't lie."

"You said you were leaving town."

"Yeah. We're gone most of the season." Each word was punctuated with another breath. "Kinda hard to do relationships that way. This is for the best. For both of us."

Or it was a lousy excuse. If she really felt that way, why had she kissed him?

But whatever. At least he knew where he stood.

They weren't dating. They weren't even friends.

They were rivals competing for the same job. One he was determined to win.

Game on.

Present day

THIS WAS NOT WHAT ORION HAD signed up for. They were going to die. Not from fighting a wildland fire though. Not that it would be any consolation to his mother. He was going to die for getting roped into Logan's rescue mission.

The wind caught Orion's parachute, jerking him to the left. Using his toggles, he followed Tori—because no one actually called her Victoria—but she was struggling. He couldn't see smokejumpers Vince and Cadee, who had jumped before them. A draft had swept them in the opposite direction. Orion needed a clearing to land in, yet they were surrounded by a thick patch of burnt spruce and cedars.

With the airplane losing fuel and going down fast, they hadn't had time to scope anything out.

There. A small patch of black ashy ground— probably rocky, but better than snagging on a sharp trunk. Especially since they didn't have their typical Kevlar suits on for this last-minute rescue.

"Tori!" he yelled, trying to point to the landing spot.

But her main canopy still wasn't deploying. His heart stopped until her RSL activated, pulling her reserve chute. Tori's descent slowed, and Orion could breathe again. But there was no sign of the others in his crew.

The whine of ATVs in the distance grew louder. Right. Because it wasn't enough that their whole crew had flown into the middle of the wilderness to help Logan rescue Jamie and her brother, who was caught up in some shady stuff. Their plane had been gunned down by militia. Armed men who knew this backcountry and were still after them.

These first few weeks weren't turning out to be the greatest start to his smokejumping career.

And Tori was drifting. He pulled the toggle, caught the same draft. It spun him to see the airplane he'd just jumped from falling way too fast.

The other smokejumpers were miles away by now. Hopefully they all made it.

Gunshots sounded. Orion wanted to pull his own weapon out of its holster, but he needed both hands to steer and follow Tori. As soon as they hit the ground, he'd need it in hand to protect her. As it was, she headed straight for a craggy stand of dead trees, burnt from the wildfire that had just run through the area a few days ago.

He could only watch as she dropped suddenly, her chute catching on a thick limb. Her scream stopped his heart.

Somehow, he managed to drop in without tangling up on a snag. He freed himself from the chute and sprinted to Tori, gun drawn and ready in case any of the militia found them.

"You okay?" He scanned the area for threats.

"Do I look okay?"

Her usual snark was a good sign. He'd found out quickly the first day of training that neither of them would hold back as they duked it out for a smokejumper spot. The two of them had fought hard, but they'd been the newest. If it hadn't been for one of the other trainees breaking his leg during training, one of them wouldn't be here.

Jade had just never said which one. And they were both on probationary status for the first month of jumping. It wouldn't take much to lose the coveted spot, so neither one of them was backing down.

Victoria had been fun and easy to talk to, enjoyed life to the fullest.

Tori was all business.

At least with him. She joked around with the others, but during training, she hadn't let up at all. She'd met every challenge head-on. Even now that they were on the team, the temperature between them hadn't thawed. She kept to her friends, often working with Vince or Cadee. He stuck with Logan and JoJo.

But something had changed on that plane. He wasn't sad that Jade had paired them up in the few minutes they'd had to formulate a plan on the airplane that was losing fuel and going down.

Watching Logan fight to find and save Jamie, he'd seen what was most important. All of them being shot at as they'd rushed to the plane, barely taking off as the militia had tried to mow them down with rifles, had him thinking about that last night before they'd become rivals.

That night was embedded in his brain. The dance they'd shared. The kiss.

So yes, in the dark quiet of nights, the moment replayed in his mind. But this was Tori. Apparently she'd meant it when she'd said she'd given herself the one night to let loose. He'd just been a means to an end. But he didn't want to see her hurt or killed by those guys on ATVs.

"I really wish I had my letdown tape."

"I've got one." Orion set down his light pack and grabbed the strap out of it. He scrambled up the thick trunk, testing its strength as he did. It was still strong enough to hold them, thankfully. "Good thing you're not too far off the ground."

"Easy for you to say." She glared at him through the blackened spruce branches. "Just hand me the tape. With as many times as we practiced the letdown procedures, I can do it in my sleep."

He shimmied out on the limb she was caught on. "Yeah, but we don't have our suits—"

"It's fine, Orion."

Right. She didn't like anyone trying to help her. Maybe it reminded her too much of her sisters smothering her. Either way, he knew better. He dropped the line.

She looped the strap with the carabiner and rings on the harness she wore. "Do you have a knife too? You'll have to cut the lines since I need the chute harness."

"Just say when."

Once she rigged the strap to let herself down, she called up to him, "Go ahead."

"You checked all—"

"Orion! Cut me loose. Those guys on the ATVs are coming."

Fine. He cut the lines. She yelped as she dropped free of the chute. But the strap held her as it was meant to. She smoothly belayed herself to the ground.

Orion glanced out. He could hear the four-wheelers, but with the slight ridge blocking his view, he couldn't see anything. They needed to move quickly. He climbed down and stowed his knife in his cargo pants. Tori was bundling the strap when suddenly she was on the ground.

"What happened?"

She grunted. "Nothing. The dumb strap was caught around my foot, and I tripped." She stood, a grim look on her face. She took a step and almost fell over again.

Orion caught her by the arm. "Are you okay?"

Her eyes closed a second, lips shut tight. "I twisted my ankle."

"Let me take a—"

"It's fine." She took another step but needed the tree trunk to support herself.

"Stop fighting me and let me help," Orion said.

"I don't—"

One of the ATVs crested the ridge.

"Oh, for Pete's sake." Orion scooped her up and ran.

"What are you doing?" she shouted, wriggling as if she was trying to get away from him.

"Just hold on!"

She actually did what he asked and tightened her arms around his neck. Which was good since he could hardly focus on putting one foot in front of the other while navigating the slight incline, avoiding trees, and holding her.

The ATV engines grew louder, though Orion still couldn't see them yet.

"They're getting closer. We're sitting ducks out here."

She was right. With the whole landscape in black and white, their bright yellow shirts stood out.

"We need to blend in." Orion set her gently on the ground and rubbed soot and ash on his shirt. She followed his example. Her shirt was soon a charcoal gray. Once they were reasonably covered, he stood over her, ready to pick her up again.

"Seriously, Orion, I can take care of myself." She spoke through gritted teeth and tried to get up.

Too bad. He helped her stand and then swept her up into his arms.

The movies made it look a lot easier.

She pushed against him. "I'll be okay. You can put me do—"

"No time. You're hurt. We need to get away." It was all the breath he had to explain. He ran, dodging black trunks, skirting around rocks and fallen trees. If he could reach the next ridge up ahead where the land dropped away, maybe they could find a place to hide.

"Hey! Here's one of their parachutes!" a deep male voice yelled, his voice echoing through the burnt forest.

They were close.

"Tracks go this way," another called out.

Footprints in the ash would lead the men right to them. Orion picked up the pace.

"There!" Tori pointed to a thin stream cutting across the field a few yards away. "That should hide our tracks. Put me down, and I can—"

"Forget it." He made a beeline for the water.

"Orion, the ankle is fine. Let me down!"

His arms and lungs burned. Hopefully they had enough of a lead. He dropped her legs but kept an arm around her waist. "Can you stand okay?"

Instead of answering, she jogged away. A slight limp, but she was handling it. The cold mountain water soaked their feet and ankles as they ran downhill in the stream until it tumbled over a craggy edge. They stood there, sucking in oxygen and looking for an escape route.

The stream became a tiny waterfall, dropping fast down a cliff. They climbed out of the water and around the boulders that lined the cliff edge. The landscape fell away in a steep hill on one side of the water. Maybe they should try climbing the rocky ledge on the other side of the stream. But that would be hard on Tori's ankle.

The forest was once again green and alive here. They wouldn't have to worry about being tracked through the ash. But the gunmen on their ATVs were still heading their way. Orion glanced behind him, but the ridge above hid the blackened landscape from his view. He walked away from the cliff and onto green vegetation. Maybe it was—

His foot slipped in wet moss. He hit the ground, rolled down the sharp incline. Branches and brush whipped his face as he slid.

"Ry!"

He threw an arm over his face, at the mercy of gravity as he flew downward, unable to find purchase. *Oomph*. His shoulder caught a thick trunk, and his body bounced off, sliding down until finally stopping at the bottom of a ravine.

For a moment he lay there, his own ragged breath all he could hear. He tried opening his eyes. His vision blurred. Excruciating pain radiated from his shoulder and across his forehead.

That couldn't be good.

He waited for the sky and trees to stop spinning. Gingerly pushed up to a sitting position.

A groan escaped. The agony from his shoulder and the pounding in his head sent a wave of nausea through him.

"Orion!" Tori slid down into the ravine on her bottom, holding on to tree trunks and limbs to keep from barreling down like he had. "Are you okay?"

She was there, kneeling in front of him, concern in her gaze.

If it weren't for his shoulder being on fire and the probable skull fracture he had—given the way his head hurt—he'd be tempted to joke with her.

"Oooh, that doesn't look good. I think you dislocated it," she said as she assessed his shoulder.

Teeth clenched tight against the pain, he could only grunt in response. He felt along his clavicle and left shoulder. "It's still in joint." But it wouldn't surprise him if he'd pulled or torn something in there.

"And you're bleeding." Her lips thinned and brow pinched as she leaned in, studying his forehead. She searched her pockets, found a bandanna, and wrapped it around his head. "Hopefully this will stop it." She tied a knot. He tried not to wince as it tightened around his wound.

He hated being helpless like this, especially in front of her. But he was in too much pain to put up pretenses.

"Help me up." He leaned on her to stand, another bout of nausea almost taking him out again. He powered through and stood. He tried one step. Didn't keel over. Another.

"I've got this," he told Tori. She looked reluctant but stepped away.

Orion stepped up to a black spruce, rested his good hand on the ragged bark.

He closed his eyes, focusing the next few breaths to go deep.

Better.

But not great.

"Are you okay?" Tori rested a light hand on his arm.

He nodded and immediately regretted it as dizziness hit him.

"Maybe you should sit again," Tori said.

He didn't fight it. He gingerly sat and leaned his back and head against the tree. Took a moment to listen. "I don't hear the ATVs."

"I guess that's one benefit to falling down a mountain. There's no way they could get those vehicles down here."

"There are better ways to find a good hiding spot." He bit back the groan building inside. Better to focus on her. "How's the ankle?"

"I'll live." She released a short breath, blowing a strand of blonde hair out of her eyes.

Orion looked around them. It wasn't bad as far as hiding spots went, and as dizzy as he was, he needed the rest, as much as he hated to admit it.

"Can you call the team?" Tori asked him. "We need to see where they are."

She probably meant to see if Neil and Saxon had made it as they'd tried to pilot a plane with a fuel leak. Smoking. Going down. It would be a miracle if they'd survived.

"I lost my phone in the jump. Where's yours? I can make the call if you give it to me." She held out a hand.

He reached into one of his pockets and pulled out his phone. The screen had shattered, the back cracked and broken. "Guess this isn't going to help us much."

"What about the tracking rings Jade gave us?" Tori looked at her hand. "Mine is cracked. Will it still work?"

"I don't know. I left mine on base since this wasn't a fire call."

Tori swallowed. For the first time since he'd met her, he saw a hint of vulnerability in her eyes as they shifted and took in her surroundings. "We're on our own."

Sure, Tori and Orion had gone head-to-head more than once this season, trying to prove each was worthy of the smokejumper badge. And maybe as he'd beaten her across the finish line on their daily run or gotten a faster time on their drills, she'd had a moment of weakness and wished he'd developed a sudden fear of heights or an allergy to wildfire smoke.

But she didn't *really* want to see him hurt.

And he was definitely hurting now. But just as she thought they might be out of danger, the faraway engine sounds came from the ridge above.

Her breath caught. "We have to move. They're back."

Her ankle hurt more than she let on, but she still grabbed Orion's good arm. She draped it around her shoulders and hooked her own arm around his waist. "Let's go, Montana."

He grunted as they moved. "You haven't called me that since—"

"Yeah, yeah. Let's not go there."

The pain must be bad. He didn't say anything and simply leaned on her as they took tentative steps around boulders and tree roots. They followed the ravine away from the place he'd landed.

Heading east from what she could tell. "Once we lose these guys, we can head south, back to base camp." She hit her ankle on a rock and sucked in a short breath. Man, that hurt!

"You okay?" Orion asked.

"Mm-hmm." She bit down on her back molars, hard. The pain didn't pass though. She hobbled another step. Great. She'd injured it more, could hardly put any weight on it. Orion dropped his arm and took a few steps without leaning on her.

He found a sturdy branch and handed it to her to use as a crutch. "We're quite the pair. Your ankle. My shoulder and head."

She stared at the makeshift crutch a moment. Did she give in to pain, or pride?

Pain won. She took the branch. "Who are

these militia guys anyway, and why are they trying to kill us when they were only after Jamie and Logan?" Maybe she could direct her anger and ire toward the bad guys to push through.

"From what Logan said, Jamie's brother Tristan infiltrated the group that was using that burnt compound we searched a few days ago. I guess she downloaded some financial information or something when they had her captured earlier. And now we just helped Jamie and Tristan escape them. They're probably trying to cut loose ends or think we know something."

"So they shoot down our plane and are now hunting us like prey. Great. Like I didn't have enough creeps making my life miserable—" She clamped her lips tight. It wasn't Orion's problem. Why was she even bringing this up?

"What creeps? You mean me?" he asked.

"No! I was—it doesn't matter. But no. I mean, sure, you're incredibly annoying, but I would never call you a creep."

"At least, not to my face?" Even through the ash and grime covering his face, the handsome smile he gave as they hobbled along loosened some of the tension in her neck.

That was better. He was still pale, obviously

in pain the way he held his one arm tight across his chest, but a teasing Orion she could handle.

Because the moment he'd tumbled down that slope, she'd realized maybe she'd made a mistake walking away from him *that* night, the one when they'd danced under the stars. Maybe she'd made the wrong choice walking away, not seeing if their time together could've been the start of something.

It was too late now to find out. But she could dial down the rivalry a bit. They were teammates. Probably time to start acting like it.

"So really. Who's bothering you back home?" he asked.

She glanced over again. He stopped, held back a low branch so she could walk ahead of him.

If nothing else, talking would help assess if he had a concussion or brain injury.

"I'm not sure. Probably just my dumb ex. But someone is leaving notes. Smashed my windshield. That sort of thing."

"They smashed your windshield?"

"Yeah. That's why I was late that first day of training. I had to file a police report and was trying to line up someone to fix it, and let's just say it was an awful way to start the day. I was hoping to make a much better first impression."

"But that was the morning after we met."

"Yeah, it was while we were at the park that night. When I reached my car after we . . . went our separate ways, I had a note and a busted windshield waiting for me."

Orion stood straight, clenched a fist, almost like he would go to battle for her. "Why didn't you come after me? I would've—"

"There was nothing you could do." And she really shouldn't be so touched that he was so upset by this, like he really cared about her. Probably he couldn't help the desire for justice, and it had nothing to do with her.

"What about that guy on the dance floor? He wasn't happy when you turned him down. It could've been him."

"Maybe, but I don't know him. How would he know which car was mine? My guess is still my ex. Though I haven't seen him around town. Still, I feel like someone is watching me all the time. But it's probably just paranoia."

"Anything else happen since then?"

"No. But we've been pretty swamped with training and fires. Not like we've had much downtime."

"Did the police say anything?"

"No leads last I checked."

He stopped then. Leaned on a tree, his face ashen.

"Ry? You all ri—"

He spun and emptied his lunch onto the ground.

That wasn't good. Nausea and vomiting were signs of a possible concussion.

Now that they'd stopped, the stillness of the forest surrounded them. Birds and chipmunks chattered in the canopy above. The ATV engines were still audible in the distance.

"They're still looking for us," she said.

He glanced up at her and nodded.

And who knew where the rest of their team was?

She studied Orion—the sweat beading on his nose and above his lip. Right now it was the two of them alone in the Alaskan wilderness, miles from civilization. "We have to push on. Maybe find shelter for the night."

"Do you think we should try to find the others?"

"That means heading toward the militia guys. And farther away from camp."

"Yeah, let's keep moving. It's cooling off." He pushed himself off the tree and stood again. "You're probably right. We need shelter. The temps will drop overnight." They started hiking once more. "We'll share what I have in my pack. If we can find a source of water, I have purification tablets."

The hike was far slower than her normal pace. She didn't bother to hide how much she needed the branch-crutch as her ankle grew more swollen. Orion stopped to make a sling for his injured shoulder with a piece of paracord.

The thick tree cover blocked the sun, but the glimpses of sky were growing darker. Tori didn't know how much time had passed. All she could focus on was each step, getting farther from the militia and trying not to roll her good ankle.

"There's water." Orion pointed to a break in the trees where a small stream—maybe even the same one from earlier—tumbled down the mountain. From the looks of things, it had been bigger at one point. Now, with drought and lighter snowfall totals this winter, it was barely more than a trickle. But it was water.

Orion filled his canteen and dropped in the tiny white tab. "We'll have to wait for the tablet to kill everything off. We should keep going. Maybe follow this stream."

"I guess it's our best shot at finding a road or trail."

They continued on, the landscape sloping down but nothing drastic. After a while, they drank from Orion's canteen and shared a couple of protein bars. The water tasted like chlorine but better than getting giardia. The trees weren't as thick here, giving the wind enough room to chill her skin.

She rubbed her arms. "We need to find a place to hole up for the night."

They found a spot where an old birch tree growing next to a rock outcropping sheltered them from the wind on three sides.

Orion wrenched a small branch with his good arm. "I should have my Pulaski."

"It's not like we knew we'd need it when we rushed off to help Logan rescue Jamie. Besides, how would you use it one-handed?" She took the branch from him. "Let me do this. You try to find us some fire kindling."

She broke more green branches that were within reach and laid them across low limbs of their tree and the rock, creating a bit of a roof.

Orion found some dry kindling. "Do you think we should light a fire though? What if the smoke alerts the militia to our location? We don't have anything to cook. It's risky and not necessary."

But she was cold. And now that they weren't hiking anymore, the chill was settling in.

Mostly, she hated the dark.

A little fire would push back the cold creeping around them. But he was right. It would lead those ATV riders right to their position.

"If we wait until dark and keep the fire small, we'll be okay. We'll just have to take turns staying awake and making sure it doesn't get out of control." Wolves howled in the distance. She didn't even want to think about all the wildlife that was out here.

He nodded and dug a little patch of dirt, lined it with rocks, and she pushed all the dead, dry brush away.

"Ow!" Tori dropped the branches she'd cleared. A long cut ran down her palm. Not deep but bleeding. The thin gold band of the tracking ring now had blood on it. She quickly moved it from her right hand to her left.

"Here." Orion handed her a tissue from his pack. Once the cut was clean, they made a small fire so that they had some warmth but it wouldn't make much smoke, and settled in the shelter, their backs against the wide trunk and rock wall.

"You should eat something, Ry."

He shook his head. "I'm more tired than anything. Let's save the last protein bar until tomorrow. We'll need the energy to hike out. We get some rest now, and we'll be set."

His grin was strained at the corners—maybe it was pain tugging at them. He was still pale.

"I'll take the first watch. We should make sure you don't sleep more than two or three hours at a time, just in case you have a concussion."

"I should fight you on taking the first watch, but I'm beat." He paused a moment. "Do you mind if I pray for us?"

"Pray?" She balked. "Knock yourself out. Not that it will do anything, but if it makes you feel better . . ."

"Well, it certainly isn't going to hurt, right?"

She shrugged. God hadn't answered any of her prayers, but if it was important to him, she'd stay quiet.

"Lord, please protect us. Keep us safe and help us to get back home. Amen."

"That's it?" It didn't sound like the long, flowery prayers she'd heard the few times her aunt had dragged her to church.

"He knows what we need. Wake me in two hours?"

She nodded and tried to send him a confident thumbs-up. He didn't have to know her issues with the dark. Or how cold she was already, their little flame doing nothing to warm her.

Orion quickly fell fast asleep, his breathing steady and deep. A little snuffle, not quite a snore, made her smile. She scooted closer to him, his body a better source of warmth than their meager fire. She fed it with the sticks they'd collected. The wind moaned between the trees. She stirred the flames with her last branch and watched the embers glow. Something lumbered not too far away—a heavy body crashing through the underbrush.

Did fire attract animals?

In a panic, Tori threw dirt on the burning sticks. Orion didn't stir.

Some help he was.

Wait . . . would fire deter animals? Shoot. Now it was too late.

She moved closer to Orion. This was going to be a long night.

THREE

A LOUD NOISE IN HIS DREAM WOKE Orion slowly. His back was chilled, but something warm and soft curled against his chest. Drawn by the warmth, he pulled it closer.

"Wake up!" Pressure on his foot, a strange voice . . . what was going on?

Orion opened his eyes to see his good arm draped over Tori, who had cuddled up against him. She stirred.

But he was more worried about the man standing at his feet holding a knife. A bushy salt-and-pepper beard and equally bushy hair and eyebrows gave him a menacing look. Another man with dirty dark-blond hair and beard and a snake tattoo circling his neck stood next to him.

Although the man was younger, the shadowed look about him had Orion's senses immediately on alert.

Orion raised his good hand and slowly sat up. "Hey, we don't mean any harm."

Tori moaned and rolled up against his leg, shivered. Poor girl had to be freezing.

"Get your woman up." The older man jerked his chin toward Tori. The younger guy eyed her sleeping form, igniting a protectiveness in Orion as he nudged her shoulder.

"Tori, honey. Wake up." He kept his arm around her. Maybe if this guy thought they were a couple, he'd keep away from her.

She cracked one eye open, paused. She shot up to a sitting position and finally noticed the strangers standing over them. "Who are you?"

Orion crouched in front of her and moved to stand face-to-face with the men and block their view of Tori. Oh, and apparently they weren't alone. Three more men were behind them a few feet away, standing guard.

But Tori must've stood too, because he felt her small hand rest on his arm from behind him. "What's going on?"

"What are you two doing out here?" the older

man asked. His eyes narrowed as he looked Orion up and down. He must be the leader of the group.

These guys were big, fit, but there were no ATVs or big equipment like the militiamen had. Their clothes were sturdy, worn but clean. No logos or anything. All sported beards, looking almost like the lumberjacks of old—except for the one with the snake tattoo. Maybe they weren't with the militia. No one wore camo or combat boots.

But better to be safe if the militia was still after them. "We're trying to get back to Copper Mountain. We're . . . hikers. Got lost."

"What happened?" The leader gestured toward Orion's head wound. "And why dontcha have any equipment?"

"I fell, slid down a ravine. Lost one of our packs."

"Are you part of that troop running around on ATVs and shooting up the air, scaring away all the game?"

By the scowl on the lumberjack's face, apparently they *weren't* part of the militia and weren't overly fond of the group.

Orion shook his head. But who were these guys, and could they be trusted?

Tori's stomach grumbled loud enough for them all to hear.

"I take it you're hungry." The leader looked back at the others and nodded. "Come with us."

"Why should we come with you?" Tori hopped on one foot and stood shoulder to shoulder with Orion, suspicion in her eyes. "How do we know we can trust you?"

Tattoo Guy kept a lingering gaze on Tori, scanning her from top to bottom with obvious interest. And not the polite kind.

Orion didn't want him getting close to her. He was tempted to walk away and say they'd make it on their own.

The leader crossed his arms. "Look, I don't trust you much either, but we're Christian folk, and we're commanded to help the injured and the lost and the hungry. Guess you qualify. We have two canoes not far from here that we'll take to our establishment. But if you want to go out there alone, you're a good fifty miles from Copper Mountain. Go for it."

Tori looked at Orion. He couldn't read what she was trying to say. But the way his head and shoulder throbbed with searing pain, and the fact that she wasn't standing on her injured ankle, meant they were never gonna make it fifty miles without food or water and help.

Maybe they could bypass this whole thing. Orion addressed the leader. "Do you have a satellite phone? We could contact our friends and—"

"We don't have anything like that. We live a simple life, off-grid. I'm not crazy about bringing strangers in, but if you come with us, we can tend to your wounds until you're better, feed you, and point you in the right direction. Since you're married and all"—he pointed to the ring on Tori's left hand—"you can stay in one of the cabins."

Tori balked. "Oh, but we're not—"

"We're not going to turn down the help and such a generous offer." Orion threw an arm around Tori.

Thankfully, she stayed quiet, even though she jabbed him in the side with her sharp elbow.

He looked at her, raised his eyebrows. Couldn't she see he was trying to protect her? "Let's just gather up our stuff, *honey*. These men want to help."

She rolled her eyes, but thankfully, the strangers couldn't see her face. "Sure, *sweetheart*. But I need to take care of some . . . personal business first."

She wasn't the only one. Orion spoke to the

leader. "We'll be right there." Orion tried to smile through the pain.

The man nodded and went off with his buddies a few yards away.

"Why did you let him think we're married?" she hissed.

"Call it a hunch. I dunno. Thought it would be safer. Just go along with it, please."

She glanced at the men. "Fine, but don't get any ideas."

"Believe me, I learned my lesson."

After a short hike—one that still took an obvious toll on Tori by the way she relied completely on her crutch, sweat dripping down her ash-caked face—they took the canoes through a calm stretch of river.

Orion was grateful they could get off their feet but hated being at the mercy of complete strangers. He couldn't even help paddle. The river widened after a while, and they disembarked, leaving the canoes on a rack situated between two big trees. A well-worn path led them away from the river.

One of the men held a string of fish. The other had a game bag, but Orion couldn't be sure what was in it. A group of children—various ages, most of them barefoot, and all the girls wearing long skirts and dresses—met them on the path. Their hushed awe at Orion and Tori gave him an unsettled feeling in his bones. Guess they didn't get many strangers out this way.

Up ahead on the trail, there was a break in the trees and multiple log structures.

One of the older boys reached for the stringer of fish. He pointed to the game bag the guy with dirty-blond hair carried—the one who spent way too much time watching Tori.

"Hey, Jeremiah, what'd ya find in the traps?"

"Hare and grouse."

"Can I help you skin the rabbits?" the boy asked.

"Sure." Jeremiah and one of the other men branched off and left the group. The boy skipped off with them.

"You come with me," the leader said to Tori and Orion. "I'm Amos, by the way. And this is the Refuge."

Orion could see why it was called that. Protected by towering spruce and pines, the place did feel like a natural fortress.

The children surrounding and following them didn't say much, but they looked and whispered to each other as the whole entourage traipsed through the forest path to the middle of the group of buildings. It was a little slow going with Tori leaning heavily on Orion's good arm on their way up the path.

Two big log structures faced each other. Six small cabins, three on each end of the long buildings, helped create a central grassy area in the middle of the community. Beyond them were smaller sheds and maybe more cabins under the trees. A huge kettle bubbled over a fire in the center of the buildings. Women, also in longer skirts and dresses and wearing sweaters and kerchiefs over their hair, lingered around the kettle. One matron with gray hair stirred whatever they were cooking. Others stood near her with babies and toddlers on their hips. All conversation stopped as Amos led Tori and Orion to the fire.

"Hannah, these folks need help." He addressed the older woman, who stirred the kettle.

She looked at them, her lips thinning. "What exactly do they need, and why can't they find it elsewhere?"

"They're hungry, dirty, and injured. We can spare a little Christian charity, don't you think?"

It wasn't really a question.

Hannah stared them down, eyes narrowing. Then she turned her gaze to Amos. The older couple seemed to communicate silently. The man finally sighed. "Think of it this way. The sooner they're healed and fed, the sooner they'll be on their way."

Orion felt the need to smooth things over. "We don't want to bother you. I'm Orion. This is . . . Victoria."

The woman still stared and said nothing.

"For goodness' sakes, woman. They're married. No need to worry about these two. Just feed them and show them where they can clean up. Have Mara check over their wounds. I've got fish to clean."

The man stomped away. Hannah faced them both, hands on her hips. "Amos might trust you, but my trust is not so easily bestowed, and I'll expect you both to pull your weight around here. Understood?"

Orion nodded. Tori too.

"Follow me. Mara, put the babe down and come with us."

At Hannah's brusque words, a younger woman, not even twenty if Orion guessed right, handed off a tow-headed baby in a long gown to another girl, and followed them. Hannah marched to one of the small cabins.

"You'll be staying here since Hiram and his family are gone for the season. There's an outhouse outside this door." She pointed to the back wall and the wooden door off to the side. "We'll get a bath ready so you can wash yourselves off." Hannah opened the door to a small room. A double bed took up most of the space. "You'll sleep here. I'll lend you clothes while you hand Mara those filthy things you're wearing. It will take a while to wash them off and dry. You probably don't have a clue how to wash something by hand, do you?" Hannah addressed Tori.

"I'm willing to learn. I don't expect you to take care of—"

"We'll see about that." Hannah spoke in another language to Mara and then left.

Mara pulled a large metal tub off the wall and set it on the floor.

"What's that for?" Tori asked.

Mara looked at her, confused. "This is the bathtub."

Tori's wide eyes spoke volumes.

Probably this wasn't what she'd had in mind as an answer to prayer.

What kind of alternate universe had they gotten themselves into?

After drinking an herbal tea Mara made for

her and taking the most awkward and coldest bath ever, Tori slipped on a shapeless cotton dress and sweater and wool socks. She'd scrubbed with plain cotton cloth and soap that wasn't the greatest smelling but did rid her of the ash and grime, so she was clean at least. Her ankle was too swollen to put back into her boot.

Orion dumped out the water and took his own bath in the main room while she rested on the bed with the door closed.

She must've fallen asleep. When she woke, the sun was significantly higher in the sky, right above them now as Tori limped out to the tiny porch of their cabin, where she found Orion.

"Why did you let me sleep so long?"

"Figured you needed it." He had a fabric sling holding his arm close to his chest and a clean bandage around his head.

"I see someone took care of you. Shows you what kind of *wife* I am, letting someone else nurse you back to health." She rolled her eyes.

He chuckled. "Mara cleaned out my cut and bandaged it. Not much to do about the shoulder but rest it up. I was told no cutting wood for the next few days, which I guess makes me a lousy husband."

"Few days? How long do they think we're

going to be here?" she whispered as she lowered herself to sit next to Orion on the top step. Her ankle was killing her.

"Dunno. Mara is the only person that I've talked to so far. Everyone stares at us, but they seem too nervous to talk to me. And I didn't want to leave you alone in the cabin. There's too many strangers, and I don't know if I trust this group. They might be with the militia. But once I talk to Amos, we'll see about calling base camp and getting back."

"Good, because I am not a dress-and-head-covering kind of girl. We need to get back as soon as possible. See how everyone else . . . fared."

She had to believe they'd all made it and were safe. But she couldn't deny the unease in her middle. Their plane must've crashed, and the militia was out there. Had the others made it out okay?

"There he is." Orion stood and nodded toward Amos and a couple of men walking into the central area of the commune.

"Wait. I'm coming with you. In this fake marriage, we are equals. None of this little-lady stuff, letting the men make all the decisions."

"Okay." He held out his good arm.

She paused. "No push back?"

"What would I have against that? Decisions affect us both. You should be in on this."

She stared. Was he for real? Weren't most churchy guys all about women being submissive?

Well, didn't even have to be church-going men. Most that she knew were all about controlling and telling her what to do, which was why she'd vowed to never depend on a man again. And here she had to fake a marriage to survive?

"Tori, you're hurt. I'm just trying to help. You coming?" He wiggled his arm as if to remind her that he was waiting for her. "This will help us sell the husband-wife thing. It's not a sign of weakness."

She hated looking anything less than one hundred percent self-reliant and capable, but he was right. Something told her that everyone else seeing them as a married couple was vital in this little commune. With a small sigh, she allowed herself to lean on Orion as she hopped over to the fire where Amos stood with Hannah and other men and women.

"Amos, we're grateful for everything your people have provided. But if we could use a radio or satellite phone, we'll be able to contact our friends. We can be out of your hair soon." Orion offered him a hand.

Amos stared at it, looked up. "There's no radio or phone here. Thought I told you that. We live off the grid for a reason."

Okay, there was off-grid and then there was completely crazy. "You don't have any connection with the outside world?" Tori asked.

"I didn't say that. We have friends at a homestead that's a few miles away. They arrange deliveries once a month. Just had one last week."

"How do you get ahold of them?" Orion asked.

"One of us hikes over there with a list." Amos looked at them like the answer was obvious.

Orion didn't give up though. "So they have a radio or phone?"

"Yes, but you're in no condition to hike that far." Hannah spoke up.

This was getting ridiculous. Tori cleared her throat, as if she needed to announce her intention to speak. "Can't you send someone to them? They can bring back the communication equipment or pick us up—"

"No." Amos's voice shushed all conversation in the outlying groups. "There is no reason to rush. And I can't spare anyone at the moment. This time of year, every single person here is busy getting ready for winter. Cutting wood. Smoking fish. We don't work now, we don't survive. You'll stay here. Rest. Heal. When you're both better, I'll have someone lead you to the Brinks' homestead."

Orion stepped closer to Amos. "You could give us directions and—"

"Enough. I've already prayed and inquired of the Lord. You'll stay." Amos made his declaration and walked away.

Orion's mouth snapped shut. Tori didn't blame him. Probably on a good day, Orion could take the tall older man, but with his shoulder banged up and their being surrounded by men loyal to Amos, they were stuck.

One of the men who'd found them this morning looked at Tori with a scowl before walking to one of the other cabins. Probably he didn't want them here.

The feeling is mutual, buddy.

FOUR

TORI AND ORION WALKED BACK TO the cabin. As soon as they were out of earshot, Tori whispered, "Are we prisoners?"

A muscle in Orion's jaw ticked. He shut the door and faced her. "We're at their mercy for the moment. We'll need to wait a day or two until we heal, but we'll get out of here one way or another. Even if we have to sneak out."

"Maybe we can ask around to see if anyone knows where this homestead is."

"Good idea."

They were interrupted by a knock on the door.

Hannah stood on their porch. "I know you're hurt, but you, young lady, can still shell peas and help prepare the evening meal. If your husband can help you over to the dining hall, the other women will show you what to do."

"Is there anything I can help with?" Orion wasn't sure he wanted to leave Tori exposed and without backup.

"You're no good to me with that shoulder and a head injury."

"I can shell peas, at the very least."

"We don't believe in a married man, and a stranger no less, mixing with a group of women, many of whom are *un*married." Hannah's scowl did soften a bit. "But it says something that you offer."

"He could haul water one-handed." Mara came in through the open door, apparently having heard the last bit of conversation.

"I suppose he could do that." Hannah sighed. "You here to check on them?"

"Yes, ma'am. I just came from the Hoffs' place. I wanted to make sure the bleeding has stopped on that head wound and wrap Victoria's ankle."

"And the babe?" Hannah asked.

Mara's brows pinched. "He's not gaining weight. Joann is distraught."

"We'll continue to pray and trust the Lord. I'll go sit with her a spell." Hannah turned to the door. "After these two are checked over, take the woman to the dining hall and show the man to the older boys and have them haul water to boil."

With a nod she was gone.

Mara had a much softer countenance. Hopefully she would be more receptive. Orion and Tori needed an ally here.

"So, what's the matter with the baby?" Orion asked Mara as she removed the cloth bandage from around his head.

"The baby was born with a . . . gap, I guess you could call it, in his lip. I've never seen it before, and I've been at all the births here since I was twelve, but Hannah said she has, in her time before they came here and started our community."

"A cleft lip?" Tori asked.

"Yes, that's what Hannah called it. We've tried to help Joann feed him, but I don't think he's getting enough milk." Mara studied Orion's gash. "This is looking better. The bleeding stopped at least."

Tori sat down on the chair Mara indicated. "Does the baby have a cleft palate too? A gap in the roof of his mouth?"

Mara nodded. She kneeled and removed Tori's stocking. "We tried expressing milk and feeding it to him through a bottle, but he's not growing."

"They have specialty bottles for babies with

facial differences. My friend's daughter was born with a cleft lip and palate. There's even a surgery that can close the cleft when the child gets older, around eighteen months."

"Really?" Mara looked up from the ankle. "There's a certain kind of bottle for it now? He's only a few weeks old."

"Yeah, they're designed especially for them. Basically, with that cleft in the roof of the mouth, the baby can't create a vacuum for the suction to work like it would for nursing or typical bottles. But the specialty bottles use a one-way valve, so the baby just needs to use the tongue to press against the nipple and drink. There are specialists who she can see. They can help teach—"

"We don't leave the Refuge. I'm the only one with any kind of medical training, but I only know the basics." Mara wrapped the ankle in an ACE bandage.

"If we can get to the Brinks' homestead, we can get that special bottle ordered at least." Orion moved to stand by Tori.

"I don't know if we can wait that long, but I'll talk to Hannah and Joann."

"Do you know where that homestead is?" Tori asked her.

"To the east of us a few miles. I've never been, but my brother has."

"Have you lived here your whole life?" Orion asked.

Mara gently released Tori's wrapped foot onto the seat of another chair. "I think I was four when my parents joined the community."

Tori gaped. "And you haven't been away from here since? No trips or school or anything?"

"We school here. I've seen a computer and phones. When the Brinks come, sometimes they show us those bits of technology, but everything else I've learned from others or from books."

"Do you like living here? You're not being held against your will or anything, are you?" Tori asked her.

"Sometimes I dream of going to school to understand medicine more, but I know it's not possible. I don't want to leave my family. And I do love this community. We all rely on each other. If I were to leave, I would be taking away my knowledge of herbs and medicine. The Refuge needs me." Mara smiled at them, then packed the extra bandages in her small basket.

"But what if you could learn more to help them?" Tori was getting fired up now.

Mara sighed. "I don't know. I'm sure it's strange

to you, but there's something about depending on God and depending on the people around you that I love about living here. Do you have that where you are? Hannah and Amos talk about how godless modern society is."

Orion and Tori looked at each other. Tori's expression said, *This one is all you.*

"In general, they're right. But we both work as wildland firefighters. We were separated from our team. We'd really like to get back to them as soon as we can. Will you help us?"

Mara's gaze shifted to the door and back to them. "I'll help you heal as quickly as I can. The rest is in the Lord's hands."

Tori rested a hand on Mara's slim shoulder. "Will you tell that mother about the bottles? This baby has every chance at living a healthy, happy life if he can be seen by medical professionals. He doesn't have to suffer from the long-term effects of his cleft palate and lip."

"If it were up to me, I'd take baby Josiah there in a heartbeat, even if it meant leaving the Refuge for a time. But it's not up to me."

"You'll tell her though?" Orion asked.

"Yes. But I'd better get you over to the dining hall for dinner prep before Hannah comes after us." Mara helped Tori stand.

And Orion could hopefully scope out more around the commune as he helped haul water. The rest of the team had to be worried and wondering where they were by now.

No one would ever call Tori domestic.

She was better suited to rescuing people and battling wildfires. Or training people at the gym and helping them reach their potential. Yet here she was, stuck in a weird commune kitchen and surrounded by women who seemed to thrive on homemaking skills. Skills Tori did not possess. But she refused to be a freeloader, so she was determined to learn.

Tori pried open the green pod and pushed out the peas with her thumb the way the young teen on her right, with freckles and long, dark hair, showed her. Gabby had made it look easy.

Actually, all the women, even the little girls sitting at the table across from them, were helping and much faster than Tori.

"You do this every day, for every meal? Cook for all the men while they get to traipse about?" Tori kept her voice low. An older woman, Constance, supervised them all from the stove, where she stirred a huge pot, releasing the savory aroma of a fresh vegetable soup. She didn't seem the type to appreciate that kind of question.

Gabby just giggled. "They're not traipsing about. They're working too. They hunt and fish and provide a lot of our meat. They provide the wood to fuel our boilers, and the water we use. They're pretty handy to have around. And men like yours sure are nice to look at."

"Gabby!" Her friend on the other side of her, with curly brown hair and a sweet round face— maybe her name was Rebecca?—blushed bright red. "You shouldn't talk like that about a married man. Or any man!" She whispered and looked around like she wanted to make sure no one else had heard.

Constance called from the stove, "Back to work, girls."

Gabby didn't seem bothered. She swiped another pod and giggled again. "Well, it's true. Her husband *is* handsome."

Rebecca rolled her eyes. "Remember what Hannah said? 'Handsome is as handsome does.' And if it weren't for the whole community doing our part, we'd all suffer. So yes, to answer your question, us girls and the women do most of the cooking every day for the community supper. But we do the earlier meals in our own homes, and my dad and brothers help with those."

Rebecca continued to diligently work while Tori fumbled to shell the peas. Four more teens stood along the counter of the kitchen area and kneaded bread, which Gabby told her was for tomorrow. Today's loaves were fresh from the oven and cooling off, releasing a yeasty fragrance.

It certainly smelled better than a squished protein bar or working out in the sweaty gym. So maybe there was something to say for all this domesticity. Still, despite the mouthwatering scents reminding her how hungry she was, she was ready to be back at base camp.

"So, how did you meet Orion?" Gabby didn't break her shelling rhythm. Rebecca glanced up, a hint of curiosity in her gaze.

But oh, how innocent they both seemed. Had Tori ever been like that?

"Well, we met . . ." Could she use the word *saloon*? Would they even know what that was? "We met at a restaurant. Someone backed into me, and Orion caught me before I could fall. And then later, he asked me to dance."

Gabby sighed. "How romantic."

The girl wasn't wrong. Tori relived the moment more than she would ever admit. Dancing with

Orion, she'd somehow felt free and protected at the same time, as if knowing he watched over her meant she could go farther, do more, and not worry. Too bad the real world didn't work that way all the time.

Before Gabby could ask more questions, a group of guys entered the dining hall. Without being asked, younger boys took benches off the long tables and set them on the floor.

"Guess that's our cue." Gabby grinned and pulled Rebecca away. They carried stacks of plates to the tables and, with some of the little girls, began setting places. Gabby immediately started up a conversation with one of the teen boys as she worked.

"That's good for now." Constance took the bowl full of fresh green peas from Tori. "You can move to one of the tables and wait for the meal. Do you need help?"

Tori shook her head. She hobbled out of the kitchen area into the dining hall. She found an out-of-the-way spot and sat while the rest of the dining hall quickly filled. Everyone pitched in to set food out and ready the space. The chatter and laughter filled the room. They looked so happy. So peaceful.

Tori, on the other hand, was so out of place.

Her family dinners had usually been something her older sisters had thrown together and gobbled down as they dragged her from one sport or after-school activity to another while their father worked.

Jeremiah stared at her from another table. Tori shivered. What was it about that guy that set her on edge? He sat with three other men but didn't talk much.

Finally, Orion walked in and found her. "You okay?" he asked. And she was grateful for a familiar face.

Her whole body relaxed. "I'm good."

He sat next to her, and another young couple soon settled across the long table from them. Amos stood at the head of the table, and the room hushed immediately. Everyone bowed their head as he prayed. And as soon as he sat, the room buzzed again with conversation. Tori tried to ignore Jeremiah and his creepy vibes.

The food was a great distraction. Orion passed her a dish of butter, and she slathered it onto the still-warm bread. Tori took a sip of soup just as the woman across the table, with a blue bandanna in her hair, smiled and asked, "Do you two have children?"

Tori almost spit out the soup. Instead, she

swallowed it in one gulp, which only burned her tongue and set off a coughing fit.

Orion dropped his spoon. "Uh . . . no children for us . . . yet. Haven't been married long." He handed Tori a glass of water. "Are you all right, hon?"

She nodded and took a long draw from the glass, trying to stop her throat from seizing. *Please, someone change the subject.*

"Well, don't worry. When your time comes and the good Lord blesses you with children, you'll have your hands full in the best of ways." The woman beamed at the man next to her.

He nodded. "We have a quiver full, that's for sure. We outgrew our little cabin and had to build a new one last year."

"How many kids do you have?" Orion asked.

"Six. And one more on the way." The woman rubbed her swollen belly. "Those cabins you're staying in are called honeymoon cabins for a reason. They're for the newly married and young married couples. You're in the right place."

"They're cozy for more than one reason. You'll conserve heat and learn how to work together, for sure." The man slurped his soup.

His wife nodded. "That small bedroom is nice

for cuddling on the cold summer nights since we don't heat the cabins this time of year."

Orion stilled. "They're not heated?"

"Not when we can help it. We want to conserve the wood for the winter when we really need it." The woman took a dainty sip and continued. "There should be plenty of blankets and quilts, but"—she leaned forward and kept her voice low—"we find body warmth is best."

Her husband chuckled.

That was it. Tori might need to find a place outside to sleep tonight. She shoved a big piece of bread into her mouth.

Tori tried to finish her food quickly. Hannah excused her from helping with the cleanup and suggested Tori and Orion turn in early. Tori would've taken off in a dash if she could've, but it was rather slow going, leaning on Orion's good arm to get to their cabin.

"We need to get out of here." If she sounded like she was grumbling, so be it.

"Easier said than done. You can hardly walk, let alone hike miles and miles."

Tori huffed. "We don't belong here. *I* don't belong here. If these people knew me at all—"

"Hey." Orion stopped, faced her, and rubbed his warm hands down her chilled arms. "We'll get out of here. And I promise, I'm not going to let anything happen to you. I bet after a good night's sleep resting that ankle and my shoulder, we'll be strong enough to leave soon."

"We better." Tori looked off into the distance. Strange animal sounds from the dark forest beyond the river only added to the uneasiness setting her on edge.

"We just have to pretend a little longer. Come on, *honey*."

Maybe it was the teasing challenge in his voice or the crooked grin, but either way, something settled deep in her bones.

If she had to be stuck anywhere, being stuck with Orion at least made it better.

FIVE

OH, HE WAS IN BIG TROUBLE.

Standing in the middle of the commune with the low sun shining down on Tori's blonde hair, the feel of her slender arms under his fingertips as he tried to comfort her, had Orion forgetting all about the agony of his shoulder and the throbbing in his head. He just wanted Tori to feel safe.

And it would be for the best if he could forget that pesky kiss they'd shared on the night they'd met.

Tori never seemed rattled to jump out of a plane at three thousand feet or to face down a raging fire. But in this backwoods community,

94

even now, knowing they were a peaceful group, she was more spooked than he'd seen her.

Maybe it was just the thought of pretending they were married. Which weirdly didn't freak him out like it probably should. If Orion were ever to marry, it would hopefully be to someone as strong as Tori, with her tantalizing mixture of fun and fierce. But it needed to be someone who shared his faith too. And Tori had made it clear that she didn't.

So he really needed to watch himself. Especially when all he wanted to do was hold her in his arms again. And here, like the couple across from them at dinner had shown, everyone would probably cheer them on.

"Come on, let's get settled for the night. I'll sleep on the couch, and you can have the room."

And maybe he should dunk himself in the cold river first.

As they walked to the cabin, others milled around in the evening breezes. The Alaskan summer sun wouldn't set for quite a while. Everyone seemed to enjoy the fresh air. Kids ran around, playing and giggling. A few couples sat in the grass, watching them. No one was in a hurry to turn in. But Jeremiah stood on the porch of the dining hall, leaning against the log post and staring at them.

Staring at Tori.

Orion would definitely be locking the cabin door and checking the windows.

In the little log cabin, Tori brewed an herbal tea from a mix Mara had given them. Orion found a stash of quilts in a closet. He took one of the pillows from the room and made himself a bed on the couch of the of the small living area while Tori left to use the outhouse one more time. Orion wished he could light a fire in the stove that nestled in the corner between the living area and bedroom. The air was already chilly. Maybe he could—

A knock on the door interrupted his thoughts.

Shoot. He grabbed the pillow and blankets he'd just laid out and threw them into the bedroom. If it was Mara, she would want to come inside.

But it wasn't Mara. Instead, Amos stood at the door with another man and a young teenage girl. "Sorry to bother you, Orion, but this here is Hiram and his daughter Abigail. They came back earlier than we expected."

Hiram? Oh. "This is your cabin." Orion backed

away from the door to allow them in. "We can go somewhere el—"

"No need." Hiram smiled through his bushy beard. His eyes crinkled in the corner, giving him a jolly Santa-like appearance. "I would bunk with the bachelors, but there really isn't a place for Abigail and my wife to stay. My wife is just catching up with Hannah. She's here too."

Tori came in the back door and walked over. Orion made introductions and explained the situation.

"Orion and I can sleep on the floor somewhere. Even the dining hall if needed." Tori leaned on the chair closest to the door, staying off her sore ankle. Even though she smiled at Abigail and Hiram, it wasn't nearly as bright as her usual grin. She had to be tired and in pain.

"My wife would skin me alive if she found out I put a young couple like you on the floor. She won't hear of it, and neither will I." Hiram pointed to the loft area above the living room couch. "If you don't mind, Abigail and Belinda can sleep up there in the kids' room. I can make a pallet on the floor with them. Then you two can have your privacy."

"Looks like it's all settled, then." Amos clapped Hiram on the shoulder and left.

What were they supposed to say?

Fatigue and pain were getting the better of Orion. It made for a good excuse to suggest he and Tori turn in early. After awkward goodnights, he and Tori slipped into the bedroom.

She sank onto the bed and carefully stretched out her foot. She closed her eyes tight, pain etched into her features.

"How's the swelling?" Orion laid out one of the quilts on the floor. Thankfully, a rug would provide some cushion and warmth. The chill in the room had him wishing for a roaring fire in the stove out there.

"It's actually going down. I mean, it hurts, but it's already getting better staying off it today and having it wrapped."

"Hopefully we can convince them tomorrow to let us go to that homestead and call the team." He fluffed the pillow and laid it on the floor next to the quilt he'd found.

"Ry, come on. We're adults. We can both sleep on the bed. I promise I won't make any moves on you." Humor tinted her voice. It was nice to hear her sounding more like herself finally.

"Nah, I'll be fine down here. Besides, I bet you're a bed hog. I'd probably end up down here anyway." No need to let her know that it wasn't her restraint that he questioned.

It was evening, but the sun still shone in the window, lighting the room. Orion moved the thick curtains over the opening, darkening the room instantly.

Tori's light gasp stilled him.

"You okay?" he asked her.

"Yeah, I guess I didn't realize how dark it would get in here." Her chuckle fell flat.

Without asking, Orion cracked the curtains so a sliver of light showed. He'd prefer it pitch black, but something told him Tori would rest easier this way.

"Thanks," she whispered.

"No problem. Sweet dreams, Tori. Don't worry. We'll get out of here soon."

"G'night, Ry."

He must've fallen asleep in a flash, because he awakened suddenly, a strange sound rousing him. A whimper came from the bed.

"Tori?" he whispered. He sat up, but she didn't respond.

The room was completely dark now, which meant it had to be between midnight and four a.m. He was about to lie back down when Tori cried out.

Orion jumped up, barely making out her silhouette as she sat in the middle of the bed.

"Hey, you're okay." He moved to sit next to her. She crawled into his arms and nestled there, shivering. He pulled the blankets and tucked them around her. Orion could feel her rapid heartbeat. What was going on?

He smoothed the hair off her forehead and leaned against the headboard. He didn't know what had freaked her out, but he whispered into the darkness, "Tori, it's all right. I'm here."

"It's all right. Everything's fine." Her shaky voice repeated his words a few times until her breathing slowed to a normal rhythm. Eventually, her death grip on his shirt loosened, and she sat up on her own.

Orion found her hand and gently stroked her long fingers, hoping his presence would bring her a sense of calm. "You okay?"

"I am now." She squeezed his hand. "Sorry to wake you."

"What's the use of having a fake husband if he can't be useful once in a while?"

She released a breathy chuckle. "Right. But I don't think you signed up for this. To help me fight my demons."

"Actually, I think that's what fake husbands are best at. At least, the ones that are friends too."

"Yeah." She leaned against the headboard next to him. "The dark . . . it just gets to me sometimes."

Orion didn't say anything.

Eventually Tori rested her head on his shoulder. "When I was little, I would sleepwalk and get night terrors. I'd wake up in strange places. Usually it was just the hallway or the kitchen. But once I woke up in the neighbor's yard."

"That had to be freaky."

"I was so scared. I've never known darkness like that. It was too dark for me to recognize where I was."

"Were you far from your own house?"

"Three houses away. In a backyard I'd never seen. I have no clue how I got there. All I know is I went to bed in my own room and woke up to pitch blackness and strange sounds, and I was outside."

"What did you do?"

"I cried. I prayed so hard for my dad to find me and take me home."

"Did he?"

"No." She choked on the word. "I sat there in the dark. Alone. For hours. I was paralyzed with fear. It felt like that night was never going to end."

He pulled her in closer, thinking of the lost and terrified little girl, praying for a rescue that had never come. The image sent a pang through his chest. "How did you get home?"

"Eventually daylight came, and I found my way to the front yard and back to my own house."

"You were gone all night? My mom would've freaked. What did your parents say?"

"My mom died when I was a toddler. I don't remember her." Tori sniffed. "And my dad didn't say much. He was barely around. He did add some high locks to the doors outside, though, after my sister Penny yelled at him. But ever since, I've hated the dark. I've never been able to shake off the terror of that night." Her body shuddered.

Orion wrapped his arm around her. "Well, no wonder. I can't imagine being lost in the dark like that. I probably slept with a nightlight until I was in high school." He tried to lighten the mood with a quiet chuckle.

"You can make fun of me. I know it's silly, a grown woman afraid of the dark."

"It's not silly at all. You're one of the bravest people I know. I mean, look at what we've already come through."

She didn't say anything, but she relaxed against him, the tension in her posture melting away.

"Ry?"

"Yeah?"

She paused. "Would you stay here? Just for the night."

"I'm not going anywhere. Go ahead and try to get some sleep if you can."

She mumbled something that sounded like "Okay," and fell asleep quickly.

Orion didn't. He remembered the night they met. The way she'd danced and twirled under the twinkle lights. He remembered her gentle touch when she'd helped bandage his wound in the forest. Somehow, the weeks of intense rivalry didn't seem so important. He was falling for her. And that wasn't good.

He prayed until dawn that he could remember this was only a fake marriage.

The place might be called the Refuge, but it felt more like a prison.

After twenty-four hours stuck at the commune, Tori's short handle on her patience was quickly disintegrating. She couldn't get rid of the constant gnawing inside, wondering what had happened to the rest of the Midnight Sun crew. Had the militia gotten anyone? Had everyone made it out of the plane crash?

And if Orion asked her one more time if she was okay, she might resort to violence.

Which totally wasn't his fault. Like on the night they'd first met, he'd been nothing but a gentleman. Maybe it was the embarrassment of her late-night confession getting to her. She'd completely fallen apart like some dumb damsel in distress. She was supposed to be stronger than that. But he hadn't brought it up this morning when they'd woken.

She and Orion walked back to the cabin's front porch from the chapel building. Apparently, morning prayer time was nonnegotiable to stay here. At least she didn't have to lean on Orion anymore to get around. She hobbled on her own and sat on the log bench outside the front door. Hiram and his family were gone for the day and had made sure to tell them they could stay as long as they liked.

But this wasn't a vacation. It was time to leave.

They just needed to figure out where this Brink homestead was.

"I heard Amos tell some of the guys that they're going out this afternoon to check on their game traps. If you really think you can walk, we could try leaving when they're gone," Orion said.

"I can definitely walk. I can use a branch for support too, but we still don't know where the homestead is."

"Amos outright refused to tell me anything this morning when I told him we'd like to go. He said it's not time yet. And this morning at breakfast when I tried to ask Mara's brother where the homestead was, he made an excuse to leave the table."

"Maybe we have Mara ask him. But no matter what, we have to get back. We've been gone two days already. The team is probably worried about us." Tori kept her voice low, though the daily tasks had been given and most of the community members were off completing them.

"We don't have food or supplies to get very far if we don't know where we're going. I don't want to put Mara in a bad spot with her family, but we'll have to risk it and ask her to get her brother to tell us where the homestead is."

"What are you two whispering about?" Gabby stepped up to the cabin. She had a bit of a crush on Orion.

Not that Tori could blame her there. His dark hair, blue eyes, and those hero vibes made a very appealing package. Gabby smiled up at him now, ignoring Tori completely. "Is it stuff only husbands and wives talk about?"

"Yup." Tori linked an arm through Orion's. Better remind the girl the man was taken. "Did you need something, Gabby?"

"I'm supposed to get you to come help at the garden. Hannah said you're late."

Tori glanced at Ry. She laid a hand on her stomach and groaned a little, hoping he'd catch on.

"Oh, honey, is your stomach still bothering you?" Orion played the part well.

She nodded. "It must've been something I ate." She looked at Gabby. "Could you find Mara and ask her if she has anything to help an upset stomach?"

"Sure, but it probably won't help you if you're pregnant."

Tori balked. "There's no way I'm pregnant."

Gabby's brow wrinkled. "Why not? You're married. Isn't it time for you to start having kids?"

This was not the time to explain anything to a young, impressionable girl. "Could you please get her?" Tori bent over and wrapped her arms around her middle, groaning again for good measure.

"I'd better help her. You'll get Mara for us?" Orion asked.

"Of course." But Gabby stayed glued to the bottom step, looking up at him a few seconds still. Orion ushered Tori to the door before the girl finally slipped away.

"Great. Now the whole community probably thinks I have morning sickness," Tori muttered.

"Who cares? We're leaving." Orion shut the door behind them.

Tori paused. "I feel kinda bad lying to them."

"Yeah, but the way Jeremiah follows you around, it's safer for them to think we're married. Let's get dressed back in our regular clothes, pack the canteen with boiled water, and see what food we can scrounge up." He unbuttoned the thick flannel Hiram had loaned him.

Tori found her pants clean and folded on the table. She slipped them on under her long dress. "I also hate the idea of stealing from them."

Even if the older ladies watched her suspiciously all. the. time. No surprise there since they were Christians. Weren't they all about judgment and condemnation?

Not that she got that sense from Orion though. And Hiram and his family were sweet. And when Orion had held the door open for Hannah this morning, she'd nodded with the tiniest hint of a smile. So maybe he was winning her over. But if these people had any clue about Tori's past, they'd kick her out in a flash of fire and brimstone.

Still, that didn't mean she actually wanted to take from them without asking. "I mean, they work so hard for everything they have here. I don't want to take from them."

"I don't either, but if we're going out there in the backcountry, we have to prepare for the worst-case scenario, which means we have fifty miles to hike to get back to base camp if we can't find the homestead or run into a problem there. If we can set a decent pace, I think we can do that in two days. But we'll need sustenance."

Right. But Tori had helped in the kitchen last night and seen their stocked shelves. "Most of the food is in glass jars or containers. But I think I saw some canned goods in the kitchen area. Mara said they ship in some things they can't grow."

"Find whatever you can carry easily, and hopefully we won't even need it and can leave it with the Brinks to give back to them."

"Sure. What are you going to do?" Tori asked him, averting her eyes when he shrugged off the flannel, leaving the tight base-layer shirt showing off his well-sculpted torso.

Okay, fine. She peeked.

Sheesh. She was bad as Gabby!

"I'll see if I can find something we can use as a tent and get some other supplies that might come in handy. Hurry back though. Mara will be coming to make sure you're okay."

Better leave now and let her face cool off. Tori snuck around the back of the cabins to a side entrance of the dining hall. Someone inside sang "Amazing Grace," the soprano voice lingering in the air.

Through many dangers, toils, and snares,
I have already come:
'Tis grace has brought me safe thus far,
And grace will lead me home.

Wishful thinking there. Grace had never done such a thing for her. She and Orion would make it home on their own, thank you.

Tori waited until the music faded away and a door closed, then she slipped into the dark pantry area. Without any lights from the windows, she pulled a few cans from the shelves and brought them to the hallway. Beans. Those would do. She stored two cans in the cargo pockets of the trail pants she wore under her dress. She grabbed one more just in case and a small package of home-made jerky, then checked the area outside the back door. All clear. She stepped into the tree line and rounded the corner, slipping behind the next-door cabin.

"What are you doing?"

Tori gasped. Her empty hand flew to her chest, and she spotted who was lurking. "Oh my goodness, Jeremiah. You scared me."

He came out from behind a tree, a scowl on his face as he studied her. "You're wearing pants."

"So what? I realize the women here don't, but it's common in many places."

"Why are you wearing them under your dress?" He stepped closer.

Instead of answering, Tori lifted her chin and moved toward the cabin where she and Orion were staying. "My husband is waiting for me. I better go."

Jeremiah was quick. He stepped up and grabbed her arm. "I asked you a question." He looked at the can in her hand. "Are you stealing from us?"

"I needed—"

"I think you might need a lesson in hospitality." He dragged her a few steps farther into the trees. Away from the cabin.

Tori dug her feet in. "I'm not going anywhere with you." She yanked but couldn't free her arm.

His viselike grip squeezed tighter. He tugged her closer to himself, grabbed both arms, and pinned her against a tree.

"What are you doing! I'm married!"

"Then your husband should keep a better eye on you." He slapped a dirty hand over her mouth as she tried to scream. He moved in close to her face, his breath like rotten meat.

Footsteps sounded. "Tori?" Orion called.

She couldn't see him, but if she made enough noise, maybe he'd come close enough to see Jeremiah. She thrashed, but Jeremiah pressed himself closer, squeezing her jaw closed. Rough bark dug into her back as he pressed her against the thick tree trunk.

But Tori was *not* going to be a victim again. She lifted her good foot and slammed it down onto Jeremiah's foot. When he backed away enough, she kneed him in the groin and shoved with all her strength. He bowled over and growled.

Tori spun and ran as fast as she could with her limp. "Ry!" Within seconds, she broke out of the tree line and straight into Orion's arms.

"What happened?" He held her in a safe embrace. She couldn't say anything at first as tremors took over her body. He scooped her up and carried her back to their cabin. "Tori, you're scaring me. What happened out there?" He gently laid her on a chair, wiped a strand of hair from her face. His brow furrowed as he studied her.

She finally caught her breath enough to whisper, "Jeremiah grabbed me."

The muscles along Orion's jaw flexed. "Where is he?"

"Ry, forget it. We need to get out of here. Now. We can't—"

A knock on the door stopped her.

"It's me. Mara."

"Do we let her in?" Orion asked. "Say the word, and I'll make up an excuse and we can leave."

But when it came down to it, she did trust Mara. And someone needed to warn the other women about Jeremiah. "Let her in."

Orion opened the door. Mara walked in, but as soon as she saw Tori, her smile dimmed. "What's wrong?"

Tori explained what had happened. "It's not that we aren't grateful, but we have to get out of here. Our team is probably worried. And I won't stay any longer with Jeremiah here."

Mara frowned. "I don't blame you." She looked around like she was afraid someone might be listening. "Jeremiah showed up about a year ago claiming he wanted to join our community. He hasn't done anything like what he tried with you, but he makes many of us women uncomfortable."

"Will you help us leave, then?" Orion asked her straight up.

She nodded.

Good, because Tori couldn't get out of here fast enough.

SIX

ORION WOULD'VE PREFERRED MORE time to prepare, but with Jeremiah nowhere to be found, their window of opportunity to leave before Amos got back was closing quickly.

With Mara's help, they found a length of canvas and some old sleeping bags in case they had to spend more time out in the middle of nowhere. Once back in Hiram's cabin, Mara had her brother John draw a map and explain it to Orion while she and Tori packed their one backpack.

"Thanks," Orion told him. "You better go before the others return. And keep an eye out for Jeremiah. When I went back to find him, he was gone. So look after your sister and the other girls."

Mara's brother stood tall. "I will."

"If you ever need anything, have the Brinks call the Midnight Sun base camp out of Copper Mountain," Tori told Mara.

"I'll be praying for you," she said.

Tori nodded, but the smile she gave didn't reach her eyes at all.

As far as Orion was concerned, it was all for the best that nothing had happened with Tori the night they met. Her discomfort with anything spiritual would've been a big point of contention.

But he couldn't deny the ache that she didn't share his faith. That was the main thing he appreciated about the Refuge. Their prayer time this morning had fed his soul. He hadn't realized how parched he had been for fellowship, worship, and truth until Amos had gathered them all in the chapel this morning. But with the militia hunting Tori and him down, every minute they stayed was another minute they put these people in danger. And most of them didn't deserve it.

Jeremiah was one he wouldn't mind leaving in the hands of the militia. Then again, the man would probably fit right in with them.

Heck, he could be one of them to begin with since he'd only shown up last year so mysteriously.

"Let's go." He held the back door open for Tori while Mara and John left by the front door.

They skirted behind the main building and found the trail they needed. The cedars and spruces they passed were scrappy but dense. Patches of sun trickled down through the canopy and lit the packed-down dirt path. Ferns grew plentifully along the way.

With as many times as the trail branched off through the thick forest, Orion was grateful for John's map. A couple hours later, they stopped for a water break.

"We must be getting close." Tori swallowed another long draw.

"I would think so. How's the ankle?"

"Sore, but okay. Mara wrapped it tight for me."

The sound of mewling stilled them. "Did you hear that?" Orion asked Tori.

"I was hoping I was just hearing things. What is it?"

"I don't know. Maybe an animal?"

"If it's a baby animal, there's probably a mama somewhere, and I don't want to get between them."

A crack sounded, like footsteps on branches.

"What if it's Jeremiah?" Tori whispered.

"Let's get out of here." He held out a hand to help her up from the fallen log she was sitting on. They jogged down the trail.

Footsteps and the strange sound followed them. Orion led Tori off the trail and behind a stand of spruce. "Stay down. We need to see who or what this is and if they're following us." He pulled out his gun and crouched beside Tori, watching the trail.

The sound grew louder. "It sounds like a baby crying," Tori said, her voice low.

She was right. But it wasn't the loud, lusty cry of an upset newborn. This cry was weak.

And another sound accompanied it. A soft lullaby being sung.

Orion put the gun in the back waistband of his pants. Anyone singing a lullaby couldn't be too scary, but if this was some kind of trap, he wanted his gun accessible.

Coming down the trail was a woman dressed like all the others at the Refuge and a man Orion had seen a few times but hadn't met. She was unfamiliar and wore a bundle in a sling, bouncing it gently as she sang. Orion watched a minute more. The couple looked worried. The man kept a vigilant eye on their surroundings, but they didn't seem threatening at all.

"Should we see what they're doing?" Tori whispered.

"Let's wait."

But the man must've heard them. He stopped and called out, "We don't want any trouble. You can come out from behind the trees."

Orion approached them, Tori right by his side. He said, "What are you doing?"

"We came looking for you," the man said. "We need your help."

"We can't stay at the Refuge. We need to get back to our home." Orion stood, arms crossed, facing the man.

"I know. And that's why we're here." The man put his arm around the woman's shoulders. "I'm Abraham, and this is my wife, Joann."

"You're the ones with the baby. Josiah, right?" Tori walked over to the woman and smiled.

Joann nodded. "Mara said there's help for babies like him. Is that true?"

"Yes. Would you like us to order those special bottles I told Mara about when we get home, and then find a way to get them to you?"

Tears ran down the woman's cheeks. "I don't think we have that long. He's gotten more and more lethargic. He barely eats now."

Abraham drew her closer. "We've tried for a long time to have children. Josiah is our first. We can't lose him." His voice faltered.

"You're the answer to our prayers." Joann's

wobbly smile among the tears tugged at Orion's heart.

"How are *we* the answer?" Tori asked her.

"I wanted to talk to you, but Mara told us you'd left. We followed." Joann swayed, holding on to the baby, rocking him back and forth.

"I need you to take Joann and Josiah and get the medical help he needs." Abraham held out a wad of cash. "I've made and sold furniture and Joann's quilts. If this isn't enough, I'll get more. But it will be easier to find food and lodging for Joann and the baby alone. And I'm needed at the Refuge if we're going to make it through the winter. Take them. Please."

Tori's eyes widened. She looked to Orion.

Baby Josiah cried again. A pitiful cry at that. It did sound more like a weak kitten than a baby. Joann pulled out a bottle and tried feeding him.

Orion didn't take the cash. "Why not ask the Brinks? It's not that we don't want to help. It's just . . . there's a militia group that we've run across. They aren't friendly. I would hate to put your family in danger."

"The Brinks are pretty removed from society too. They do what's necessary, but I don't know who they know in town." Abraham looked at Tori. "But Mara said you know someone with a child like Josiah. And like Joann said, we've prayed about this. God answered. I'm trusting Him and you to lead them and bring them back home to me. Please."

"Even though it could be dangerous? If the Brinks don't have a vehicle, we have a couple days' hike before we reach town." Orion needed to know they understood the risks.

"'Many are the afflictions of the righteous: but the Lord delivereth him out of them all.' Psalm 34:19."

Well, how could Orion refuse that? But it wasn't just up to him. "Tori? You okay with this?"

She looked down at Josiah, his tiny face peeking out of the sling as Joann fed him. His eyes were closed. Milk dribbled out of the side of his mouth. Was he getting any of it down? "I am. But we should get going."

After a tearful goodbye between Abraham and Joann, the father kissed his son's forehead and prayed over the group. "Lord, bless them. Protect them. Keep them strong for the journey, and bring Joann and Josiah back home."

The baby settled down. Tori took a pack from Abraham. "I've got this."

"I'd better get back. Amos won't be happy about this, but I need to do what's best for my family. Make sure you stay on the trail. There's lots of snares and traps," Abraham said before he turned and jogged away.

Joann wiped the tears and pulled back her shoulders. "Let's go."

It wasn't long before they spotted the brown metal roof of a building peeking out above the trees ahead. The path widened to an actual dirt road.

"Looks promising." Orion looked down at the map. "This must be it."

"Now we just have to hope the Brinks are here and have a way to get us to Copper Mountain." Tori shifted the backpack straps on her shoulders.

"Maybe you two should wait here, and I can run up ahead and check to make sure everything is safe." Orion didn't want to walk into another dangerous situation.

"I don't know why it wouldn't be safe. People from the Refuge often come here, and there's never been a problem before," Joann said.

"We should stay together," Tori agreed.

They walked into a clearing with a log house, a couple metal-sided sheds, and a little barn.

Tori spun in a slow circle, looking around. "It's a nice place. Let's just hope they're nice people too."

Goats bleated in a corral off the barn, but beyond that, it was eerily quiet. The three adults spread out as they moved toward the house.

"Oh no." Joann, her mouth agape, stared into the distance. Three chickens lay dead in the dirt outside what looked like an open coop.

"Look!" Tori pointed to the porch of the log house.

A woman lay on the wooden planks, passed out.

Tori made to rush to the woman.

"Wait!" Orion stopped her with his arm out. "We don't know what we're walking into. Joann, stay right here. Don't get any closer to those chickens."

Joann backed away, but Tori pushed against him. "We can't just leave the—"

The woman on the porch moaned.

"She's alive. She needs our help." And Tori couldn't stand to see anyone in pain and not help.

"We go together, then." Orion dropped his arm. "And try not to touch anything."

By the time they made it to the steps, the woman was rousing. Her long brown hair was pulled back in a braid, her flannel shirt and jeans dusty as she sat up, holding her head.

"Are you okay?" Tori asked her, sinking down to sit on the top step.

The woman blinked, scratched at a cluster of red spots on her forearm. "I don't know." She coughed.

"Did something happen?" Orion stayed standing and scanned the yard.

"Who are you?" the woman asked.

"I'm Tori. This is Orion." Tori gestured to the middle of the yard. "And that's Joann and baby Josiah. They're from the Refuge, and we were hoping you could help us get to Copper Mountain."

"I'm Kitri." She slowly moved to standing and looked out at the property as if searching for something.

"Kitri, did something happen to you to knock you out?" Orion asked again. "Are you in danger?"

"Buzz broomly fix gone."

"What was that?" Orion looked confused.

Kitri spouted off another meaningless string of words.

"Let's go inside and get her some water. Something is going on." Tori helped Kitri into the house. Hopefully she wasn't having a stroke. She walked normally, which was a good sign.

Orion swept up a rifle lying next to the door. "Joann, come with us." He held the door open until Joann was safely inside.

The log home was cozy. A big stone fireplace took up most of the living room, and the simple leather furniture and stacks of quilts and books scattered around gave it a homey touch.

Tori led Kitri to the small wooden table in the open dining room, while Orion searched the cupboards, eventually bringing a glass of water for each of them. Kitri stared off into space rather than taking the glass.

"Here, try to drink." Tori put the glass in her hand.

Kitri slowly lifted the glass and sipped. She closed her eyes a moment and shook her head.

"Do you remember what happened?" Tori asked.

"A drone. There was a drone, and it sprayed something in the air while I was feeding the chickens."

"Do you remember having that rash before the drone?" Orion pointed at her arms. The angry red welts on her skin covered the backs of her hands up to her elbows.

Kitri shook her head. "No. I remember rushing up the steps for the gun, but I must've passed out."

"Where is the rest of your family?" Joann tucked the sling tighter around Josiah.

"Fishing. It's our annual salmon trip. They'll be gone a couple more days. I stayed to take care of the animals and the garden." Kitri set the glass down and scratched her arm again.

"I think you need medical attention. We need to get back to Copper Mountain. You should come with us." Orion didn't sound like he would take no for an answer.

"I can't leave the animals."

"If that drone sprayed something on you, the first thing you need to do is wash it off. Do you have a shower?" Tori asked.

Kitri nodded. "I'll go wash off."

"Do you have a radio or satellite phone?" Orion asked as she stood.

"Sat phone is over there on the counter. But it isn't working. I was waiting for Cameron to get back and look at it. It won't charge."

"I'll see what I can do." Orion walked over to the counter. Kitri left the room. He checked it over.

"Anything?" Tori stood next to him.

He tried pressing buttons. Nothing happened.

He checked the battery on the back, removed it, and tried the extra battery sitting on the counter. "Still nothing. Not sure what's wrong with it."

Joann spoke up from the table. "Should we be worried about whatever that spray was? Do you think it's still in the air?" She held the baby closer, patting his back and rocking.

"I don't know. But if it killed the chickens out there and knocked Kitri out, it can't be good." Tori fiddled with her ring.

"Maybe we should bring one of the chickens with us to test for chemicals." Orion set the useless phone down.

"Do you really want to expose all of us if whatever is on them is still active? We can always tell the authorities and send them back here. The important thing is we get Kitri and Josiah some medical attention." Tori refrained from shivering. The thought of something dangerous in the air was downright terrifying. An enemy she could see was an enemy she could fight. But who knew what had been sprayed? Or why. "We should leave as soon as possible."

"I'll go see what vehicles are available." Orion left out the front door.

"Josiah?" Joann gently lifted the baby out of the sling. He didn't stir or cry. She tried dripping water on his feet. "He's not responding. And he hasn't had a wet diaper all day." She looked up at Tori, panic in her eyes.

"Can you get him to drink anything? Maybe he's dehydrated."

"My milk in the bottle probably isn't good anymore."

"Let's try a little sugar water." Tori ransacked the cupboards until she found sugar. She mixed some with water and brought it to Joann. Together they dripped a few dropperfuls down his tiny mouth. He wriggled but didn't open his eyes.

"He's getting weaker." Joann's voice wobbled.

Orion came in. "What's wrong?"

"We need to get Josiah to the clinic ASAP."

Orion dangled keys in the air. "There's a truck ready to go. All the animals have water. So far it looks like just the chickens were affected."

Kitri stumbled into the room from the hall.

"You okay?" Tori asked her.

Her dark hair dripped water and was a little tangled, but at least she had clean clothes on. The T-shirt showed the rash up and down both arms.

"Dizzy, but—" She looked at Tori, rolled her eyes. Not in an attitude kind of way though. They rolled back and forth rather than focusing on

Tori, who stood right in front of her. She didn't finish her thought.

"There must've been some sort of neurotoxin in that spray. We're going to get you to an emergency room."

Kitri's gaze settled on Tori for a moment, and she nodded. She allowed them to escort her to the truck, where Orion already had Joann and Josiah settled.

It was a long, bumpy ride on the dirt road that probably only the Brinks used, but no one complained. No one said much of anything. Thick forest lined the road, letting in little sunlight in this area. Joann hummed a song, maybe a hymn—it sounded familiar. Tori wouldn't begrudge her finding some comfort wherever she could with her baby suffering.

But this was why she didn't buy into the whole God-and-grace thing.

Then again, she'd heard a little here and there but never actually tried to pray herself. And the way Orion, and even Abraham, had prayed today hadn't been a bunch of religious words. It was like they'd simply been talking to God.

Couldn't hurt to try.

You say to pray, so fine. Why should Josiah suffer? He's an innocent baby. And Kitri? She didn't do anything to deserve an attack. Please, just save Josiah and heal Kitri. If You really do care, get them back home safely like Abraham prayed.

Oh, and I will never take for granted a hot shower or indoor plumbing again!

Tori breathed easier when Orion turned the truck onto a familiar paved road.

Civilization.

Within another hour, they pulled up to the small clinic in Copper Mountain. Orion offered to call the authorities for Kitri as soon as he could get a phone.

"Joann, do you want me to stay with you?" Tori asked.

The wide-eyed woman merely nodded.

They walked into the lobby. The space was small, crowded with just a few padded chairs and one coffee table with magazines scattered across its top. But the big windows facing the street displayed the mountains to the north.

"It's so bright," Joann whispered, taking everything in with wonder and maybe trepidation as they moved to the front desk. A woman in scrubs sat behind a counter.

"Can I help you?"

"Will you explain?" Joann whispered to Tori. "I don't know what to say."

Thankfully, the woman behind the counter understood the urgency, and they were rushed back. It was a good thing Tori was there. Joann looked like she was going to faint as the nurse and doctor took Josiah, examined him, and started an IV.

"What are they doing?" she kept asking. "Are they hurting him?"

Tori tried to explain the best she could and held Joann back from reaching for her baby. "We need to let them work. They're helping him. He needs fluids, and since he's not drinking, they're putting fluid directly into his body through the IV."

Another nurse came in. "Why don't you two go get a drink or something to—"

"I'm *not* leaving my baby." Joann planted her feet and stared down the nurse.

Whoa-boy. That mama-bear instinct must be kicking in.

"She's fine, Shawna. Let her stay by her son." The doctor looked up at them. "It's a good thing you brought him in now."

"Will he be okay? Do we have to go to Anchorage?" Tori asked him.

"It's your lucky day. I'm a pediatric specialist *from* Anchorage. Just came to fill in for Dr.

Hughes this week while she's gone. Josiah is weak, but—"

At that moment, the baby arched his back and cried. Finally.

"—looks like this little guy is a fighter."

Joann closed her eyes a moment, tilted her head up to the ceiling. She looked back at the doctor with shimmering eyes. "It's not luck that brought you here. It's an answer to prayer."

SEVEN

ORION COULD FINALLY CATCH HIS breath. Tori and Joann were back with the doctor. Kitri was talking to Deputy Sheriff Mills while they waited in the lobby for her turn with the doctor. Now he needed to let the team know he and Tori were okay. He excused himself and went up to the front desk.

"Could you call the Midnight Sun smoke-jumper base camp? My partner and I have been missing and need to let them know where we are."

She looked up the number and dialed, handed him the receiver.

"Midnight Sun jump base. This is Tucker—"

"It's Orion."

"Orion? Thank God! Everyone's been worried. Where have you been? Where's Tori?"

"Tori's with me, here at the clinic in Copper Mountain. We ran into some people that needed help. And we could use a ride, but not sure how long we'll be. I don't have a phone."

"Obviously. You two gave us quite the scare. Jamie couldn't get anything off your tracker rings."

"I know. I left mine at base, and I think Tori's broke. But what about everyone else? Did everyone on the plane . . ."

"Took Vince and Cadee a day to get to a phone and call in, and Neil should be released from the hospital today, but everyone is good or they're healing. What happened out there?"

"Long story. The gist of it is, a small off-grid community took us in. We didn't have a way to contact anyone. And then there was a drone attack on a homestead."

The woman behind the counter raised her eyebrows.

Oooh. This might not be the best place to talk. They didn't need to incite panic in the general population. "So, anyone free who can come get us in Copper Mountain?"

"Sure. I'll send one of the smokejumpers, but

right now they're out in the middle of something, so it will probably be a few hours."

"Sounds good. I don't know how long the doctor will take anyway, and we'll need to make sure these two women with us are settled. So we're not going anywhere."

"As soon as you're back, I want a full report."

"Will do." Orion hung up as Kitri was called back by a woman in scrubs. He went over to the deputy.

"You saw this drone, by any chance?" Deputy Mills stuck his thumbs in his pockets.

"No. We came and saw Kitri passed out on her porch. The chickens outside the coop were dead. The other animals I saw seemed fine. Someone needs to check it out though. There's a small off-grid community called the Refuge not far from the homestead. They're peaceful people. I would hate for them to be targeted."

"The Refuge? I think the sheriff's heard of them. We'll look into it. Got a number where we can reach you if we have more questions?"

"I don't have a phone at the moment, but you can find me at the Midnight Sun jump base."

Mills wrote down the info and left. Orion let his head fall back against the wall and closed his eyes. With the adrenaline of everything that had happened fading, a bone-deep weariness sank into him.

At least everyone was safe. The weight of having to protect three women and a baby was not a light one. He stretched out his legs, tempted to put his feet up on the coffee table, but he refrained, thinking of all the times his mother had scolded him for having dirty shoes on furniture.

He must've dozed off, because the next thing he knew, Tori was rousing him. "Hey, sleepyhead."

Orion rubbed his eyes. "Hey. Is Josiah—"

"He'll be okay, but they need to monitor him overnight, and Joann is going to stay with him. But for the moment, she's okay, so I'm going to walk over to my apartment and shower. I might burn these clothes when I'm done." She pulled the collar of her shirt and shuddered. "And I'll bring some food when I come back. Want anything?"

"Tucker is sending someone to get us. Should be here in a couple hours or so to take us back to base camp."

"I don't know that I should leave Joann overnight. I had to show her how to use a flushing toilet. And where's Kitri?"

"Back with the doc, I assume. Haven't heard anything." Orion stood and stretched his arms.

His shoulder ached. "I'll go get food . . . except I don't have a wallet on me. It's at base camp."

"Why don't you come with me? I'll grab my debit card, and you can use that to get us some burgers while I take the hottest shower possible and wash my hair three times."

"So basically, you're saying I should take my time?" Orion chuckled.

"Exactly."

They walked out into the cool evening. The brisk air tousled Tori's blonde hair.

She glanced at him. "Thank you for everything you did out there. If it weren't for you, I'd probably still be stuck in that tree in the middle of the bush."

"You know, for a fake married couple, I think we did all right."

She chuckled. "Yeah, as fake husbands go, you're not so bad. Guess we make a pretty good team." They waited at an intersection for a muddy truck before crossing. She looked at him. "And I'm sorry."

"Sorry about what?" Orion asked.

"I'm sorry I didn't tell you about joining the smokejumping team when we met. I just—"

"It's okay. I get it. It's hard to make the team,

and you had to focus. And I wasn't the best team player as we were battling it out for that spot."

"But out there, I knew you had my back. If I had to be stuck with anyone—" She shrugged at him and smiled. "I'm glad it was you, Montana."

Montana. Memories of their kiss swirled through his mind. Without thinking, he opened his mouth. "Is there any chance—"

She reached out her hand like a crossing guard stopping traffic. He knew that look from the night they'd met. The look she'd given him right before she'd told him they should leave things the way they were.

"Never mind." Seriously. What was he thinking? It wouldn't work out between them.

But it didn't stop the ache inside at that truth.

They reached the little downtown area of Copper Mountain. Tori led him through an alleyway that ran along the Last Frontier Bakery. Her car—with a new windshield, apparently—was parked behind the building.

"I see you got your windshield fixed. Have you had any more issues or threats? After all, I am your husband. Do I need to go out and put some hurt on someone?"

She laughed. "I haven't had any problems since

training started. If my ex was here, he's long gone by now, probably."

Tori used a magnetic hide-a-key hidden in a planter against the back of the building.

"So, you live in a bakery?"

"There are two apartments *above* the bakery. I rent one of them." She led Orion up a set of stairs and to one of the doors on the second-story porch that ran along the back of the building. "I get to live with the smell of fresh-baked bread and coffee. It's amazing."

"I bet." Orion looked out at the mountains in the distance. "Not a shabby view either."

"Right?" She leaned over the rail and breathed deep. "I don't think I'll ever tire of this."

The content look on her face brightened up ... everything. She lifted her face to the sun, letting the light cast a glow around her. Orion had never known such beauty. But before she could catch him staring at her, he looked away. Sitting against her door was a withered bouquet of roses and a long skinny box wrapped with a bow.

"Looks like someone sent you roses. They must've been here a while since they're all shriveled up." Not that Orion had any right to the sudden haze of green that came over him. He and

Tori had only pretended to be married. She could date whoever she wanted.

But Tori didn't look happy to see the flowers. In fact, her tanned skin had gone rather pale.

"I don't know, but usually my neighbor brings packages in while I'm gone." She bent down and picked up the roses. "No note. And—ouch!" She stuck a finger in her mouth. "Great. As if I needed another cut."

"Thorns?" Orion took the bundle from her while she inspected her wound.

"Yeah. One of many reasons I've never been fond of roses."

Orion barely caught the muttered words. "Maybe the gift will be more thoughtful. It looks like it could be a necklace or something."

She lifted an eyebrow. "Maybe."

She opened the lid of the box and froze. The contents spilled out and clattered on the porch planks.

There, at Tori's feet, lay a knife covered in dried blood.

A shock of cold—almost like being doused with a bucket of ice water—ran over Tori. But she didn't want to fall apart in front of Orion. It was bad enough she'd woken him up last night with her stupid nightmare. It wasn't his fault the messiness of her life kept coming back to haunt her.

"We need to report this." His words helped waken her from the stupor.

She averted her gaze from the bloody knife. "Not until I get my shower."

Yeah, it was dumb, but she needed to take control here.

Hold it together, Mitchell.

Tori tried to stop her hand from shaking as she inserted the key in the lock. Orion scanned the parking lot and the area around them before following her into the apartment.

"Who would do this to you?" Judging by his tone, Tori had no doubt Orion would take down whoever it was if they were here. Probably his inner Captain America talking.

He set the dead roses on her little dining room table, right inside the door. Neither of them touched the knife.

She bent over to unlace her boots, grateful her hair created a curtain hiding her face. "Probably the same creep that wrecked my windshield."

"Your ex-boyfriend?"

She nodded and plopped down on her couch. "He used to buy me red roses."

Orion sat next to her. Didn't say anything, but she appreciated the warmth of his presence.

She laid her head back and stared at the ceiling.

Maybe she should tell him. Just get it out. Then he'd see that he really had lucked out when she'd walked away from him that night they'd met. That a hero like him had no business with a girl like her.

But she'd never get it out if she looked at him, so she kept her focus on a small crack in the plaster above her. "I could blame it on the fact that my mom died when I was really little, like I told you before, and my dad kinda wasn't around much. He died my senior year of high school, but the sad thing is, I barely knew him when he was alive."

She swallowed and sat up. Orion still didn't speak, but he listened. He listened with his whole body. She didn't feel any judgment or censure coming from him.

She continued. "My sisters were the ones who took care of me until they moved out. And they have life figured out. I mean, Libby is married and has two adorable kids. She's successful, and her husband works all over the world. My sister Penny was an ATF agent and is now a PI, and she recently helped rescue a governor and his family. But me? I'm the screwup who got sent to the principal's office weekly and has jumped from guy to guy since middle school. And I guess . . . I was lonely. So I was easy pickings when I met Razor at a night club I was way too young to get into."

"He's your ex?"

She nodded. "He was part of a gang, a bottom-feeder dealer. But I didn't care. For a little while, I belonged somewhere. I didn't even mind that he was possessive and controlling. I thought he was being protective. And . . . I dunno, it was a messed-up way of feeling like someone cared."

"So you were part of the gang too?"

"Not really. I didn't want much to do with his friends, but I knew about the illegal stuff. I stayed out of it for the most part, I just didn't want to be alone. But when Razor was going to go to prison after shooting a guy, he moved up here to stay off the grid so the cops couldn't find him. I came with him."

"That's what brought you to Alaska?"

"Yup. But he worked the crabbing ships and was gone for weeks at a time. I needed money, so I got a job at the gym. I loved it. One of the girls there taught me how to be a trainer, and I met some good friends. I started seeing what real life could be. That being alone wasn't so bad and I was actually able to take care of myself. Every day I got stronger, pushed myself to my limits physically, and it changed my mentality too. And I started getting repeat clients. I was helping them, and that felt good."

"Then what?"

"Eventually, Razor came back from one of his trips and said the coast was clear in California, but I didn't want to go back. I told him I was done. Done with him. Done with that life."

"I'm guessing he wasn't too happy about that."

"Not at all, but I wanted to live my own life. He eventually got the message, said he could do better than me, and left. But apparently, he's back." She fiddled with the ring on her finger. She switched it back to her right hand. "I did so much with him that I regret. Whatever he wanted, I didn't argue. I don't want to be that person anymore."

"You're not. I've never known a woman stronger and more sure of herself than you." Orion's steady gaze bored into her.

And he didn't shrink back at what he saw. Instead he moved closer, gently tucking a wayward strand of hair behind her ear. She couldn't allow herself to lean into his touch.

"You don't really know me, Ry."

"I know enough. You care about people. Like

Joann and Josiah. You're strong. Courageous. And determined."

His words pierced through to the soft, tender places inside. But they were dangerous. She couldn't forget what she'd escaped. And she certainly couldn't fall for someone else, especially someone with faith.

So she'd better make sure Orion understood.

"Look, I've done so much I'm not proud of, but I'm making my own way. I know you believe in God, and you have to know that I won't be joining any kind of church. It's just another sort of gang as far as I'm concerned. Some of the meanest people I knew growing up were the Christians in my school."

"I'm sorry that was the case for you. Is that why you tensed up during the prayer time at the Refuge?"

"Probably. One of my boyfriends had very religious parents. His mother was awful. She told me straight to my face that her son was to have nothing to do with me since I was destined for hell. The funny thing is, he's the one that taught me how to hotwire a car and how to find the good parties near the college campus. He wasn't a nice guy. Yet she claimed I was the one who corrupted him."

"That's awful."

Tori swallowed at the softness in his voice. "The worst of it was after my dad died. People at his funeral, Christians and good church-going folk, whispered about how he deserved it since he was always drunk. That it was God's grace he died that way and didn't take anyone else, since he died in a one-car accident." Tears spilled down her cheeks. "I know he wasn't the greatest father and all . . . but he was still my dad."

And if that was God's grace, she didn't want anything to do with it.

Orion didn't say anything. He simply opened his arms to her, and she fell into his embrace. It was safe there, a safe place to release the hurt, the pain inflicted so long ago.

He whispered close to her ear. "What those people said about your father was wrong. That's not God's grace, Tori. God is called the Good Shepherd for a reason. He heals the sick and seeks after the lost. He loves us enough to die for us, because He came to save us. Not condemn us."

Something in her quickened at Orion's words. But she was well acquainted with people looking and sounding good on the outside and being filled with evil and corruption on the inside.

She slowly sat up and sniffed. "I don't think

those people got that message. They were really good at condemning." She reached for a tissue. "But enough of that. I just wanted you to know where I stand when it comes to all this God stuff."

"Okay."

She waited for him to say more, but it didn't come.

"That's it? You're not going to try to change me? Convince me your God is the right God?"

"That's not my job. If you do want to talk about it, I'm here."

Somehow, his answer cooled her ire. And maybe the whole faith thing did deserve some of her attention. Orion was different in a good way because of his faith. And then there were the people at the Refuge. Except for Jeremiah, they worked together for the good of the group and really seemed to live out what they preached— even if Amos was a little grumpy and Hannah had been skeptical at first. Mara was sweet and had gone out of her way to help them. Joann and Abraham trusted them, and Hiram's family had given up their bedroom, wanting Tori and Orion to have the best place to rest.

She needed some space to think.

And a shower.

She stood and pulled her hair out of its ponytail. "I'm going to take that shower now. But here—" She walked over to her purse on the desk and pulled out her debit card. "Take this. Could you grab us some food from Starlight Pizza down at the end of the block? They should let you call the sheriff from there too."

Orion hesitated. "I'm not sure I should leave you here alone. What if that guy comes back?"

"I'll lock the door behind you. But I need to clean up and get back to the clinic. I don't want to leave Joann alone for much longer."

He seemed reluctant, but Orion finally left, promising to find some food for them and be back to walk to the clinic together.

Tori tried to shake off the creep factor of Razor and his "gift," but even with the steaming hot water of the shower, she couldn't push back the chill that had settled in since seeing the knife.

She hated to admit it, but Orion's presence did give her a sense of calm protection. Not that she could give in to it and rely on him. She'd thought guys were safe before and found out the hard way that her instincts when it came to men were so skewed she couldn't tell light from dark. It felt good to get clean though—wash away the grime of two days in the wilderness, wrap herself in a fluffy towel, and slip on clean clothes. She grabbed her comfiest sweatshirt and joggers and made a cup of coffee.

Wrapped up in her fuzzy throw, she jumped at a knock on the door. She stood there a moment. Should she open it?

"Just me."

Orion.

Tori blew out the breath she'd been holding and opened the door.

He held up two bags of food. "Deputy Mills said not to touch anything else and to meet him at the clinic. He's going to send someone to collect the knife and the box. They'll check it for prints."

They walked back to the clinic and spotted the same deputy that had been talking to Kitri earlier leaning against the front desk in the lobby, clearly waiting for them. He got up and walked over. "Ready for your statement?"

Tori nodded. She moved to the far side of the lobby with the deputy, while Orion chatted with the nurse who'd come in.

Twenty minutes later, Tori finished explaining about her delivery and walked over to Orion.

"The nurse said they want to send Kitri to Anchorage for further testing and tox screens," he said.

"Is she going to be okay?"

"Dunno. I guess she has moments of being completely lucid, and then she's back to speaking gibberish. They arranged transportation and were able to get ahold of her husband and kids on his satellite phone on their fishing trip."

"Good. I'll go and check on Joann and bring her some food."

"I'll wait here for you." He passed off the bag of food and gave her a reassuring smile.

She went back and found Joann, who held Josiah close as a nurse showed her how to use a specialty bottle to feed him.

Joann smiled up at Tori. "He's eating."

"Way to go, little man." Tori ran a light finger over his downy hair.

"He's doing it. Praise God."

Tori wasn't sure about the praising God part, but the peace and joy in Joann's face was a beautiful change. "He's doing great." Tori sat in the chair next to Joann.

"They helped me express milk with a machine, but there's one I can do manually. And the doctor said when Josiah gets older, we can do that surgery you mentioned. There's even a ministry that does it for children around the world. We might qualify for their help."

"That's incredible, Joann. I'm so happy for you."

"Thank you for being God's answer to my prayer." Joann smiled with tears in her eyes, grabbing Tori's hand and squeezing tightly. "He's good, isn't He?"

Tori didn't have the heart to tell her she wasn't anyone's answer to prayer. She didn't want to dim this woman's happiness.

But God *had* been good to Joann, and Josiah had the help he needed. So maybe there was hope.

But there was a lot more evidence of darkness in this world, including her own past. So what could she do about that? Especially when it had come back to taunt her.

EIGHT

AFTER BEING WITH TORI ALMOST constantly for the last forty-eight hours, it felt weird to Orion to go their separate ways. But here he was, riding back to base camp with Cadee and Vince—who apparently were getting along really well for a change, maybe too well—while Tori stayed in Copper Mountain with Joann at the clinic overnight.

The difference in these two since the last time he'd seen them was astounding. What on earth had happened to Cadee and Vince the last couple of days?

Orion didn't like leaving Tori in town. Especially after all she'd shared with him. Losing both parents. Razor. Horrible church experiences. No wonder she'd been leery of God and anything to do with faith. Looking out at Denali in the distance, he wished she could see the vastness of the One who'd created the mountains, and more so, the depth of His love.

Lord, help her to see the truth of who You are and how much You love her.

"You need anything before we leave town?" Vince asked from the driver's side.

"I'm good. Even grabbed a new phone before you arrived." Orion held up the box to show them, but they were too busy making puppy eyes at each other to notice. "And thanks for coming to get me."

"It worked out. Everyone else was busy, but we had some follow-up police business here anyway."

"Police business?" That didn't sound good.

"It's a long story. Got tangled up with some militia guys, and it led to more trouble, but it's fine."

"So what else did I miss at base camp?" Orion asked the couple. He was definitely getting some third-wheel vibes. He needed to keep the conversation going, or Vince and Cadee would continue sneaking glances and smiling at each other.

"We've been grounded until we get another plane, so we've been busing out with the hotshots. Saxon has been working on a backup plane though. If they get it running, we'll be back in business." Vince glanced back in the mirror.

"And everyone made it okay with the plane crash?"

"Saxon managed to get Neil out of the plane after it hit the ground, which was a miracle all on its own, though Neil's condition is still serious. Logan and Jamie are working to track stuff down with the militia and figure out what they're doing. Her brother is still out there. You and Tori were the ones we were worried about. Everyone else made it back to base camp before nightfall the day of the crash, though it took us a little longer." Vince reached over and held Cadee's hand.

Cadee turned around to face Orion. "And what Vince is totally glossing over is that while you were gone, he was arrested by the FBI for embezzling funds. But it was actually an old co-worker of his from the DEA who was involved in a real-estate slash money-laundering scheme and was framing him."

"Wow. You guys have all the fun without me."

"So what about you and Tori? What happened out there?" Vince seemed eager to change the subject.

Orion explained what had happened after their jump. "With the militia chasing us, I ended up falling down the side of a mountain. Tori and I had some minor injuries." No need to mention the possible concussion or shoulder now that he was feeling better. He told them about the Refuge and how Joann and Josiah had ended up with them.

"Then we hiked to the homestead and found that it had been sprayed by a drone, and the woman that was there needed help. Drove them all to town, and you know the rest of the story. Oh, except that, apparently, Tori has a crazy ex who's leaving creepy gifts and threatening her."

"You told the sheriff, right?" Vince asked.

"Yeah, talked to Deputy Mills about the drone attack and Tori's stalker."

"Should she be staying in town alone with a stalker around?"

"Believe me, I had this discussion with her. But you know how stubborn she can be. She didn't want to leave Joann and the baby. The only reason I agreed is that the deputy promised to keep an eye on the clinic tonight, and if Josiah is strong enough to be released tomorrow, Tori wants to bring Joann and the baby out to base camp until we can get them back home."

"So you and Tori are good now? Everyone said Vince and I were the ones at each other's throats all the time, but I always thought it was you guys who couldn't get along." Cadee gave him a suspicious look.

That's probably what everyone on base had thought with the way Vince and Cadee always went head-to-head. They'd certainly been more vocal about their conflict than him and Tori.

There was something about their time at the Refuge, pretending to be married, that he didn't want to air out in front of everyone. He wanted to tuck it away in a special place, protected.

"We didn't tear each other apart, and we made it out of the wilderness alive, so yeah. We're good." But he couldn't deny he wanted more.

He wanted to be there for her. And he wanted to keep her safe. Somewhere in the last two days, they'd gone from being competitors to being allies, even friends. But more than that, he wanted her to know God's grace. To experience it herself. It tore him up inside that she'd been so hurt, that she was blinded to the truth of God's goodness.

"That's good," Cadee said. "You and Tori actually seem like a good fit as far as partners go. I think that's why Jade couldn't decide which of you to cut. Then Colson broke his leg, and she didn't have to decide."

Partners.

He liked the sound of that. Work partners, who had each other's backs. Of course, he couldn't shake the thought of that kiss they'd shared the night they first met, but that was best left in the past. Kinda hard to build a life with someone who didn't share the same faith. But he *could* help find the guy who was harassing her and keep her safe.

Not that there was time to contemplate such a thing once they reached base camp. As they drove in during the late, sunlit hours, light reflected off the Quonset huts and metal-sided hangars. The foothills in the distance guarded the area, casting a long shadow over the runway.

In the men's cabin, it was his turn to shuck the clothes he'd been wearing and clean off the last forty-eight hours' worth of sweat and dirt. He walked across the runway to the mess hall. The aroma of JoJo's chicken and wild-rice soup had him salivating.

"Nice to see you alive and well." Logan walked up and gave him a bro hug, slapping him on his back. Orion tried not to wince at the contact with his sore shoulder. "You had us worried."

"Yeah, you can't get rid of me that easily." He grinned through the pain as he gently rolled his shoulder.

"What kind of mess did you get caught in?

Tucker was saying something about a commune?" JoJo set a big bowl of soup in front of him, and the others joined them at the table.

Orion told the story between bites.

Jamie stood and grabbed a pen and paper. "Where was this homestead? The one with the drone attack."

Orion pulled up a map on the phone she handed him and backtracked his route from Copper Mountain. "Here. It was in this area. The Refuge, the commune where we stayed, was a few miles west of it."

Jamie wrote something down. She left the table without saying a word.

"What was that?" Orion asked.

Logan stood, ready to go after Jamie. "I think she's going back to the big map over there." He pointed to the other side of the room. "We saw one at the militia compound with numbers and codes. If I'm right, she's comparing the location of that homestead to the map from the militia. I'll go check on her."

After everything they'd gone through, Orion couldn't blame him. He felt the same about Tori.

"When Cadee and I were out there trying to get back to camp, we ran into a bunch of dead salmon in one of the creeks. I wonder if that has anything to do with this." Vince took his dishes, as well as Cadee's, to the kitchen.

"Lots of weird stuff is going on out here." Grizz, a man built like the bear he was nicknamed after, took another bite of soup.

Jade stood and addressed the room. "Let's not forget we're here to fight fires. People depend on us, so let's not get distracted. We've got another team of hotshots out there mopping up, but if something flares up, we need to go." She moved over to Orion. "Ready to get back in the game if we get called out? You mentioned some injuries."

"I'm good."

"You sure I don't need to find a replacement? Not that we even have a plane yet, but if you need time off—"

"No. I've had enough time off." Sure, his shoulder was killing him at the moment, but after a good night's sleep and some pain meds, he could work on exercising and strengthening it before he needed to jump again.

And he just happened to know a good trainer that could help.

Tori parked her old Honda Civic in front of the Rock gym.

"So why are we here again?" she asked Orion as they walked to the entrance. "Not that I mind. Now that Joann and Josiah are settling in at the base camp, I feel like I can get back to something resembling normal life."

"They're definitely in good hands. Who knew that those Trouble Boys were such baby freaks? Kane rocked Josiah to sleep in a matter of seconds."

"And can you believe Hammer with his 'Trouble' tattoo saying 'goochie goochie goo,' trying to make an infant smile?" She adjusted her duffel bag. "Oh, and I got word from Kitri. She was cleared from the hospital in Anchorage. Besides the weird eye-rolling tick and a lingering rash, she's okay and anxious to get back to her homestead."

"Is she going back soon?" Orion asked as he held open the door of the gym for her.

"Yeah. They still don't know what the spray was, but officials have been up there and tested everything. They said it's safe, so her husband is going to pick her up tomorrow. They'll take Joann and the baby back to the Refuge too. With the new bottles and a handheld pump to express milk, Josiah should be set. He's already gaining weight, and Joann is going to come back for a checkup in a couple weeks."

"Good." Orion didn't say anything else.

"So . . . why did you want to work out here instead of the weight room at the base camp?" Tori stared him down.

"Like I said, I wanted to come to town to check in with the sheriff's office in person. Make sure there was nothing else at your apartment."

"Yeah, but we did that. We could work out somewhere else."

They walked into the open gym. A row of treadmills and elliptical machines ran along the wall of windows facing the mountains. The smell of disinfectant and sweat was familiar, as well as the clink of weights and the running fans. She stopped at the empty front desk and faced Orion.

He looked down at the counter and picked at a piece of tape holding down the paper schedule. "I wanted you to run me through a workout for my shoulder. It's still sore, and I thought the machines here would be safer than the free weights out at base camp. But I need to be back to normal before we jump again."

"So you don't want the others to know you're injured?"

"Not until I know how bad it is. I've had this

happen before in high school, and it's already a lot better. I just need to strengthen it since it's been over a week of doing nothing."

She frowned. "Which is what a body needs to heal. You should really have a medical professional check it out."

"You are a professional. So you can check it."

"I'm a fitness trainer. I have no physical therapy experience. And I have no way of knowing if there's damage to tendons or ligaments or muscle."

"Tori. Please. Just put me through the paces. If you don't think I'm up to snuff, I'll get it checked out. But give me a shot. Why pay big bucks to some doctor if I just need to do some exercises?"

His earnest plea, and probably those big blue eyes staring into hers, went straight to her good sense and turned it to mush. "Fine, but you're going to tell me why it's so important that you're willing to take the risk of fighting fires with a bad shoulder. You shouldn't be jumping out of an airplane with a parachute if you're hurt."

She moved behind the desk to get the paperwork set to start Orion's membership.

"Hey, you're back? I thought you were off until fall." Callum, one of the gym's owners and resident handyman, came from the break room. He gave her a hug. "I've had a lot of members upset that you're gone for the season."

"That's odd, since I let all my regular clients know I wouldn't be here. They've all been assigned to other trainers." She smiled, wondering who was giving him a hard time that she was gone. "But I found you a new customer. Thought I'd get him signed up and show him around. Don't worry, I won't punch in."

Callum laughed. "Wouldn't care if you did. You're worth every penny. A lot of people are here because you're good at what you do. You have the right amount of push and concern that helps our clients reach their potential. So . . ." He slapped Orion on the shoulder—his good one. "I leave you in good hands." Then he walked over to a woman struggling with the rowing machine.

"See." Orion grinned. "I'm in good hands, like he said. So lead on, trainer."

She showed him to the shoulder press and set it at the lowest weight. "Let's see how you do. But you have to be honest with me about your pain level."

He sat on the bench and pushed the bars up. He didn't wince, but he did press his lips together tightly. She watched his well-defined muscles contract and release.

As a professional, she had no excuse for the warmth pooling in her middle as she continued studying Orion's physique. She pulled her hair back off her neck and threw it in a messy bun with her hair tie. "It's warm in here."

"Is that why you look flushed?" Orion looked concerned.

Which only made her cheeks heat even more. Time to redirect. "So why does this job mean so much to you?"

"It's my legacy. My grandfather was a smoke-jumper back in the day."

"It's nice that you want to make him proud."

"I never had the chance to meet him. He died fighting a wildfire when my mom was young. But where I grew up, everyone knew about him. Told me stories of his courage and bravery. Until last year, I didn't know who my father was, so I grew up wanting to be like my granddad."

"I get that, not knowing your dad, but why this way? Why being a smokejumper?"

Orion did a few more reps before responding. He dropped his arms and shook them out. "Because when it counted, I *wasn't* brave."

"What do you mean?" She led him over to a different machine to work on lateral raises. He didn't say anything for a while.

"Come on, Ry. I shared my shameful past. Nothing you say can top that."

He glanced at her and sighed. "In junior high I had some not-so-great friends. I justified it by thinking I could be a good influence on them, but that wasn't the case." He used his forearms to push the levers up.

"Got into a bit of trouble?" Tori's eyes caught on his biceps and lateral deltoids showing off their perfection thanks to the fitted athletic shirt he wore.

"Yeah." He did a few more reps on the lowest weight setting. "Cutting class and doing dumb pranks. But the worst of it was the time we rode our bikes to an old barn. Bobby stole cigarettes and a lighter from his dad. I knew smoking was wrong. I grew up at a camp dedicated to fighting forest fires. I knew how flammable that barn was. There was dry, old hay in the loft and all over the ground. I should've said something. But I didn't. I was too chicken."

"Did it catch fire?"

Orion allowed the weighted bar to drop. "Burned to the ground and almost killed a firefighter who was trying to put it out. All because I was too scared to do the right thing."

"I might know a little about that. I think I was

so worried about being left out or left alone that I got caught up in all sorts of situations. Were you caught?"

Orion slowly nodded. "I've never seen my mother so disappointed." He looked up at Tori, so much shame and sorrow in his gaze. "She made me go to the hospital to see the firefighter who was injured and apologize. He had burns over half his body. I've never seen someone in that much pain. And it was my fault."

"Aw, Ry, you were a dumb kid. We all do dumb stuff. It's not like you meant for the fire to happen or for that man to be hurt."

But Orion didn't look her in the eye. He stared out the window. "I haven't been able to get his words out of my head though. He said, 'I thought Jack Price's grandson would've known better. Think about what kind of man you want to be before it's too late. Your mother deserves better.'"

"So you've been trying to make up for it since?"

"Something like that. And of course, my mom blamed *herself* for my stupid choice and the fire. Which made it so much worse. I was the one responsible. Not her. So I want to prove to my mother that I can be a man she can be proud of, like my granddad. This is how I can do that."

"That's a lot of pressure to live up to. I'm sure

your mother and your grandfather, if he were alive, would be proud of you, even if you weren't a smokejumper. They'd be proud of you because of the kind of man you are, not because of the rescue work you do."

He was one of the kindest, hardest-working men she'd met. A real hero. Couldn't he see that?

"What about you? Why are *you* so adamant about being a smokejumper? Aren't you trying to prove something to your sisters? To all those people who said you were bad or weak?"

Was that what she was doing?

"I only want to prove something to myself. That I can do hard things on my own. Because I've been there. I've been on my own and scared out of my mind. Every fire is a battleground, and I want to fight to win. To help others so they won't have to fight alone."

"Seems like you help a lot of people here too though. What about that work?"

She loved working here, but it wasn't hard. And she needed to stay strong. Challenged. But rather than answer his questions, she moved him on to do delt flies. Orion sat on the bench and grabbed the bars in front of him.

"Keep your elbows straight and swing your

arms out to the side." She watched him do a full set.

"Let's see your range of motion." Tori indicated for Orion to stand. She took his arm and had him test his range, push and pull against her hand, trying to ignore how good it felt to be close to him, how different it was to work with him compared to anyone else.

"Tori! I thought you were gone." Damian, one of her regulars, came over, a white gym towel hanging from his neck. "Does this mean I can sign up for some sessions with you?" His eyes narrowed slightly as he looked at Orion for a beat.

"Oh, I'm not back. At least, not for good. Just helping out a friend here."

"That's too bad." Damian smiled at her.

It didn't do anything for her. Not like Orion's smiles that made her feel like dancing and twirling to music.

Stop comparing him to everyone else! You can stand on your own two feet, Mitchell.

She made introductions and answered another question for Damian. Since she was there, she gave him a few pointers with his workout routine and then went back to Orion.

"Be honest. What's your pain level with the exercises?"

He wrinkled his nose. "About a three. Which is nothing a little ibuprofen won't fix. And I doubt a doctor will say anything different."

If they could even get to an orthopedic doctor. He'd probably have to go to Anchorage for that. "Are you sure?"

"It feels sore, but the exercising and stretching were fine. I'll keep working on it."

"And you'll tell Jade if you don't think you can do the job?"

"I can do the job."

"Good." But could she trust herself working with him? Now that she didn't have the rivalry driving her, she was falling for him way too fast.

And he might be hero material. But that only meant that he deserved more than what she could offer.

NINE

I T TOOK A WEEK TO GET CALLED OUT again. A week for Orion to repair his shoulder. A week of working with Tori at the gym. A week where he told himself not to fall in love with her.

Everyone was ready for a callout. Everyone except Orion. His coworkers, all used to running on caffeine and adrenaline, were growing restless with training exercises and equipment inspections, while he was thankful for the downtime. Because as hard as he was working on that shoulder, it wasn't nearly where it should be.

But he wasn't going to complain when a small fire sprouted up. Without a plane, Orion and the other smokejumpers bused in with the hotshots and quickly had things under control. He made sure he was on ground crew, digging into the soil to remove fuel for the fire rather than being on the chain saw line. His right shoulder was strong and able to compensate for his sore left side while chipping away at the ground, but he didn't want to risk trying to hold a chain saw and pulling down huge trunks and limbs.

The pain level hadn't changed, but he was getting stronger, right? And it wasn't any worse after working the fire line, so that was good. Maybe he was worried about nothing.

According to Deputy Mills, there were no leads on Tori's stalker, and the militia was still out there, which kept him on high alert. After a day breaking a fire line, they bused back to base camp.

"Anyone wanna head into town and hit the Midnight Sun Saloon?" JoJo asked. "I could really go for some hot wings and live music."

"I'm in!" Tori gave her a fist bump as she walked into the hangar to help unload gear.

If Tori was going, Orion should be there to watch her back. There was still no word on Razor. "I'll come too."

Skye Parker dropped her pack. "Not me. I'm going home. My husband has dinner waiting."

"Aw, well, that's adorable, but not all of us have FBI-agent husbands who can cook, so count me in." Raine Josephs, one of the locals on the hot-shot crew, hung her helmet on the hook in her cubby and shook out her short dark hair. "I'm not driving, but I call shotgun."

Most of the crew decided to stay at camp or had other plans, so Orion squeezed in the back of Tori's Civic with JoJo while Raine and Tori sat up front. The forty-five-minute drive through the forest into Copper Mountain was easy. Orion let the girls chat and kept an eye on their surroundings. The workday was done, but the sun wouldn't set for hours. Hopefully, that would make it easier to keep Tori safe. He'd already studied the one picture Tori could find of Razor—real name Randal Mason. With average height and build, medium-brown hair, he could probably hide in a crowd with ease if not for the hardened look in his eyes and the tattoo of a tarantula crawling out of his shirt collar.

Walking into the Midnight Sun Saloon brought back memories of dancing with Tori. Same smell of buffalo sauce and smoked meat hung in the air. A different band played outside on the patio—someone doing Carrie Underwood covers by the sound of it. But Orion couldn't afford to let down his guard.

The girls chose to eat on the patio, which was

fine by him. The hostess led them through the crowded restaurant past the bar.

"Look." Tori nodded toward the far side of the bar. "That group is here again. The camo guys."

Great. The guy who'd harassed her on the dance floor the night Orion had arrived. And the group looked even bigger this time. All bulky men with thick beards. All wearing camouflage. All fisting tall beers and focused on the game playing on the big screen.

"Maybe they'll stay put to watch the game." But probably for the best he and the girls were eating outside and away from them.

Orion tried to cover Tori and keep her from their sight. They settled in at a table on the edge of the decking. Orion took the seat that gave him an unobstructed view of the patio and the doors leading back into the restaurant. As busy as it was, it took a while for their orders to arrive, but the girls didn't seem to mind. Tori relaxed, laughing at Raine's story about growing up in the back-country.

The band started playing Shania Twain's "Man, I Feel Like a Woman."

"I love this song!" JoJo jumped up. "Come on, girls." She pulled Tori and Raine onto the dance floor.

Tori came back though. "You coming, Orion?"

"I don't know how to dance, remember?"

She laughed. "We both know that's not true. If you recall, you had an excellent teacher."

That twinkle in her smirk almost had him, but someone needed to stand guard. To protect Tori of course, but also his own heart. "Go ahead and have fun. It's easier for me to keep an eye on everything from here. I'll hold our spot."

"Come on, Tori!" Raine called from the crowd.

Tori looked at Raine and then back at Orion. "You sure, Ry? I could stay with you if you want."

"Go dance. That's why we're here. I'll watch your back."

Her grin shining down on him was reward enough as it lit her eyes. "Okay, it will just be a few songs. I promise."

Orion kept his word and watched the crowd, but it was a little disconcerting how often his gaze wandered back to Tori. Hands up in the air, singing with abandon and swaying to the music, she was gorgeous. She stayed with JoJo and Raine, but the trio moved closer to the stage where the band played.

Not that he was surprised. Tori *was* music and action and energy. Of course she'd want to be closer to the source of it all.

A few songs turned to five, and by then, Orion felt bad hogging a table when a big group of people hovered around the entrance waiting for a seat. He stood and told the server they could clear the spot. None of the girls had purses, but he grabbed Tori's jean jacket and Raine's vest and stood at the edge of the dance floor.

"Ry, really you should come join us." Tori came up to him, holding her long blonde hair off her neck and fanning her face.

"*After* we take a run to the ladies' room." JoJo hooked arms with Tori and dragged her away, following Raine back into the restaurant.

"I'll wait here," Orion said. They probably didn't hear him, but as a group, they should be safe.

But fifteen minutes later, he was starting to worry. He walked back into the restaurant, past the bar and down the hallway that ran along the side where the restrooms were.

A line of women waited outside the door, so maybe it was taking a while and he was nervous over nothing. But he'd wait here to make sure he didn't miss them. He stood guard in the hall. Three more women exited the restroom, but no sign of his friends.

Finally, JoJo and Raine came out, smiled at him.

"You didn't turn her down, did you?" JoJo asked.

He didn't really care that he didn't know what she was talking about, because panic started creeping down his spine. "Where's Tori?"

Raine's grin fell. "She's supposed to be with you. Dancing."

JoJo looked around, worry lines on her forehead. "Yeah, she said she felt bad leaving you alone out there, and she didn't need to go, so she turned right around and didn't even go in the restroom with us."

Orion checked his watch. That had been over twenty minutes ago. "Split up. Raine, take the patio. JoJo, check the restaurant and bar area. I'm going outside. We'll meet back at the entrance."

Without waiting to see if they agreed or not, Orion sprinted through the crowd for the front door.

Shoving his way through the families and groups still waiting to be seated, he made it outside. More people loomed in the parking lot, but there was no sign of Tori.

Tori didn't think much about the drink the server gave her on the way back to the patio. She said it was from "the guy at your table holding your jean jacket," and Tori *was* parched from all the dancing.

She downed it quickly and set it on the bar. Maybe she should return the favor. Poor Orion would be waiting at the edge of the patio, holding their stuff, watching for threats, and keeping them safe while they danced.

Tori dug her debit card out of her jean pocket and pushed her way to the bar top. "Hey, Vic, can I get Coke and two Diets?" Raine and JoJo were probably thirsty too.

"I'm down a bartender, and it's a busy night. Got six orders in front of ya, Tori."

"I can wait." The line to the bathroom went halfway down the hall, so it wouldn't matter if it took a while.

"Tori! What are you doing here tonight? It's after seven." Evie, with her blonde hair flowing down her back in waves and her favorite cowgirl boots peeking out from her jeans, looked ready for the weekend. She skirted around the scruffy group of guys doing shots and hugged her.

Lucy followed behind her, curly red hair piled high and freckled grin catching appreciative glances. "Yeah, thought you were supposed to put out fires, not start them. You look hot, girl!" Her two friends hugged her.

"We had a smaller fire we worked today. Now I'm out celebrating with some of the crew."

"I feel like I haven't seen you in forever. Whatever happened to that cutie from Montana back in May?" Evie sipped on a drink, something pink and fruity.

"Didn't I tell you? He's a smokejumper too."

"No way!" Lucy laughed.

"Aw, it's like it was meant to be or something." Evie's hand on her heart was such an Evie move. "So are you two together?"

"Uh, not really. I mean, he's here, out on the patio waiting for me, but we're just friends."

Lucy was catching her up on all the drama from her job at the courthouse when the hostess interrupted and said Evie's table was ready.

"Let us know next time you're in town, so we can get together," Evie called as they walked away. "Or maybe we'll see you on the dance floor!"

"For sure!" Tori spun back to the bar and caught herself before she tipped over. She grabbed the back of a chair, needing the help to keep her balance. A wave of dizziness spilled over her. Hopefully, Vic had her drinks ready by now.

"Watch it." An older woman gave her the stink eye after Tori knocked into her arm.

"I'm . . . sorry." Her tongue was heavy. Maybe she should find . . . who was she with again? Her thoughts scattered. She stumbled.

"You should come with me," a deep voice whispered in her ear. A firm grasp on her arm and around her waist held her up as her knees buckled beneath her. What was wrong with her?

Tori looked up, her head falling back. Once her eyes finally focused, she gasped. "You."

The same camo guy that had tried to dance with her that night she'd met Orion. And this time she was powerless to pull away. She could hardly keep her eyes open, let alone fight back as he carried her through the crowd and outside.

What had been in that drink?

The man took her around the corner of the building and into the parking lot.

No! She couldn't get into his vehicle. That was bad. She tried to pull away, but her muscles were so weak she couldn't even move her mouth to form words.

God, help!

She collapsed.

"No you don't." The man caught her before she hit the ground and threw her in a fireman's hold over his shoulder. The motion made the dizziness even worse. Her vision blurred.

"Hey!" A voice from farther away broke through the fog in her brain. It was familiar. Safe. "Let her go!"

Orion. That's who it was. Orion was coming for her.

She hit the ground, and the world faded to black.

Tori woke to the sound of footsteps pacing. Her stomach twisted in angry spasms. She curled onto her side, waiting for the pain to pass. The footsteps quickened.

"Tori?"

She cracked open an eye to find a dim room. Her vision blurred, but she could distinguish blinking lights on little machines next to her bed. And him.

"Hey, Ry." She tried opening the other eye. Bright blue eyes framed with furrowed brows came into focus. Orion's dark-brown hair was perfectly tousled.

It wasn't fair for a guy to have such nice hair.

"What was in that drink you sent me?" She sounded like a croaking frog. Probably looked green like one too, as much as her stomach hurt. Her head throbbed.

His hand stroked her cheek, helping ease some of the pain. "I didn't send you a drink."

"But the server ..." Tori paused, trying to gather her scattered thoughts. "She said ... you sent it."

He shook his head slowly. "It wasn't me. But after talking to people at the bar, the deputies think they have it figured out. That guy at the bar asked the server to give you that drink, telling her he was trying to help me ask you out. She totally believed him and thought she was aiding a budding romance. She feels awful now, knowing that he slipped something in it. I don't know exactly what it was, but they were able to induce vomiting and have been watching your vitals all night."

All night? "Where are we?"

"Anchorage. Raine and JoJo are here too."

"And the sleaze that drugged me?"

"It's my fault, I'm sorry. I had him, but he got away. I was too worried about you to go after him. I called for help, and by the time the deputy arrived, he was gone. But they've been working with Vic and interviewing witnesses to track him down."

She slammed her eyes shut as nausea hit her middle. A moan escaped.

"I'm so sorry, Tori." His warm touch around her hand cut through the chill in the room. Her stomach calmed.

"It's not your fault." She could only whisper the words, but she wanted so much for him to believe her. "I was so scared. I've never been that helpless in my life."

She'd thought darkness was bad, but to be completely powerless over her own body and at the mercy of an evil man? She shivered at the thought. She swallowed, tried opening her eyes again to see Orion, to remind herself that she wasn't in the darkness anymore. "But I heard you there, and I knew I was going to be okay." She tried to smile, to show him how much it meant to her that he'd saved her. "I even prayed."

"Really?" The furrowed brows relaxed, and a soft smile graced his handsome face.

"Not that it was much of a prayer. More like a panicked cry." She tried to chuckle, but it hurt too much.

"He still heard."

"Guess He did. You came to my rescue."

"You know that's all it takes, right? To cry out for Him. And He's there."

She got the sense the conversation had taken a deeper turn. "You really believe that?"

He nodded, dropping a sweet kiss to her hand, still wrapped in his own. "I do."

Maybe Orion was right. She definitely needed a rescue. "I'm tired."

So tired. Tired of being afraid. Tired of trying to do life on her own, keeping it all together. Tired of trying to outrun her past. She'd been searching so long to find a *place* to belong. Maybe it really was a Person she'd been seeking this whole time.

A tear dripped down her cheek. She felt like that little girl who'd been so scared at night. Searching for a safe place, she'd tiptoe into her father's bedroom only to be sent back to her own bed. She'd sneak into one of her sisters' beds, which was fine until they woke up and kicked her out too, leaving her on her own, fighting back the darkness and fear. "Is there room for me, Ry?"

"He wants you, Victoria. There's always room."

"I'm afraid of the dark."

"He is light. And He's not going to leave you or push you away. He's always with you."

"Okay."

Then that's what I want. I want You, God.

Light and peace flooded her body and soul, and for the first time she could remember, she slept without fear.

TEN

ORION WATCHED TORI SLEEP, PRAYING over her.

In his mind he could still see Tori hanging over the strange man's shoulder, her arms dangling down. Lifeless. Somehow it wasn't too surprising that it'd been the same man who'd tried to force Tori to dance with him that night Orion had arrived in Alaska. Orion had yelled and broken into a full-out sprint to take the guy down.

Which might not have been the best idea, since he'd dropped Tori in his rush to get away. Even now Orion's shoulder throbbed in agony after tackling the kidnapper.

But he'd still gotten away.

At least Tori was safe now.

Where pain had etched lines into her face when she was passed out, a new sense of peace now smoothed her features into a slight smile and steadied her breath. She still held his hand, though her grip had relaxed and melted into his. He studied her fingers, slender and small compared to his big paws. The calluses on her palms were a testament to her determination and strength.

He wanted the chance to get to know Tori even more. To see if there was something to this . . . thing between them. If he'd read the room right, she'd had a pretty serious "come to Jesus" moment.

It ignited something in him that he could finally pursue and stop trying to douse.

But someone was out to get her.

And he wasn't about to sit back and let that happen.

The door opened and JoJo walked in. "How's she doing?" She nudged his bad shoulder.

He sucked in a breath. Couldn't hold back the wince.

"Ry, are you okay?"

Not really. He breathed out slowly, avoiding her gaze.

"Did you hurt yourself when you took Tori's

kidnapper down? I mean, it was a textbook-perfect tackle, but he was a big guy."

Yup, and Orion's already injured shoulder had taken the brunt of it.

Probably how the creep had gotten away so easily. Orion hadn't been able to hold on.

"Your silence is pretty telling. You better get that looked at." JoJo stood over him, hands on her hips, very much looking like an older sister.

A very annoying, thinks-she-knows-it-all older sister.

"It's fine. Just a little sore." He let go of Tori's hand, but he couldn't even shrug with the throbbing pain. So much for nonchalance. "Where's Raine?"

"She fell asleep in the waiting room. Neither of us were going to leave without knowing how Tori is doing. Now, back to the issue at hand—you're not leaving here until you see someone. Not to pull rank or anything, rookie, but if you're injured, we need to know."

"It's nothing you need to worry about." He was strong enough to handle a little pain. After everything his mom had sacrificed in life for him, after everything he'd cost her, he could push through the discomfort. It was his calling to save others. Hard to do that sitting at the base.

"We're all depending on each other while we're fighting a fire, so I'll make sure Jade knows. Might as well bite the bullet and get it looked at now."

So, older sister know-it-all and tattletale too. Lovely.

A few X-rays and one exam later, and Orion was officially on medical leave complete with a sling and pain killers, the only blessing being that nothing was broken.

Probably if JoJo didn't know him so well, he could've gotten away with it. Now he was out. Useless for the next few weeks.

But at least Tori woke up feeling almost normal the next morning. After Tori was discharged, Raine drove them all back to base camp in Tori's car. Jade looked over the doctor's orders and relegated the four of them to kitchen duty since it'd been such a long night for them all.

"Well, this is fun." Tori's grumbling while peeling carrots was the only thing Orion had to smile about. It was pretty cute the way she wrinkled her nose when she was annoyed.

"KP duty isn't so bad. We all have to take turns." JoJo stood by the commercial stove.

"Remind you of the Refuge?" Orion glanced at Tori.

"If we were at the Refuge, no way they'd let

you be in the kitchen." Tori pointed at him with the end of the carrot and then took a bite. "All because you're male."

"Which sounds rather unfair. Glad I didn't get stuck there." JoJo gave the big pot of pasta a stir and went back to grating the block of cheddar cheese. "The whole outhouse thing would've been a nightmare."

"Try bathing there. Washing your whole body in a little tub of cold water was no picnic." Tori added her carrot sticks to the veggie tray. "But to be fair, it wasn't all bad. Except for Jeremiah. That creep needed to leave. But the rest of them, well, it was different to be a part of a group where everyone took care of each other. They all worked in one big garden, ate their meals together, fished and hunted together. That part was nice. But I still don't wanna live there."

Raine continued to stir the veggie dip powder into the sour cream, listening but not saying anything. She was a hard one to read. They worked together to finish the cheesy hamburger casserole and get the dishes set.

It was homey and all, but this was not what Orion had signed up for.

Everyone settled around the tables once the casserole was ready. Orion swatted at a dumb fly buzzing around his head as he ate with Logan and Jamie and Tori. The sound of a plane engine interrupted the meal.

"It's early." Jamie wiped her mouth and ran for the door.

"What is she talking about?" Ham asked Logan from the next table over.

"Go find out."

Everyone left their dinner and moved outside. A sparkly new red-and-white Twin Otter plane taxied down the short runway.

Jade's jaw dropped. "Did you buy us a new airplane?" She stared at Jamie.

"Maybe." Jamie's grin didn't hide a thing. "You couldn't keep limping along on that rinky-dink plane even if Saxon fixed it up. And . . . I know a guy."

The whole crew surrounded the Twin Otter.

"She's a beauty." Saxon ran his hand along the sleek body.

"It'll be good to get back in the air, fighting fires." Jade looked over at Sanchez, Kane, and Mack. "Not that we don't like hanging out on the bus with you guys, but I've been on the ground too long. I'm ready to jump again."

Tell me about it.

Orion shouldn't be a baby, but how was a guy

supposed to do what he was meant to do when he was grounded with a dumb injury?

"Who's that?" Mack nodded toward the entrance of the camp, where a black truck drove up.

The decal on the side of the vehicle said "Sheriff."

It wasn't Deputy Mills, who'd taken their statements earlier. This time it was the sheriff himself who walked over. "Nice plane you got."

"You should come up with us sometime, Deke." Skye opened up the door in the back of the plane and stuck her head in. "This is amazing. It even smells brand new."

"That'd be nice and all, but I need to talk to Ms. Mitchell," the sheriff said.

"We can go in the mess hall. Do you mind if Orion comes too?" Tori asked. "If it's about the guy from last night, Ry will know more than I will. My memory is really spotty."

"That's fine with me."

They settled at a table with coffee. "Have you found anything yet?" Orion asked.

Sheriff Starr took a sip before answering. "The guy who tried to abduct you is Wayne Osborne. Got him on camera slipping something into your drink. The rest of his crew doesn't know much. One of them said Wayne mentioned being hired to do something illegal, but no one is fessing up if they know more. All that to say, we're on the lookout for Osborne, but there's a good possibility he's not behind the delivery, just the abduction. He could've been hired to do someone else's dirty work."

"Is he with the militia that tried to shoot us down in the airplane? Since getting caught up in trying to help Logan save Jamie, it's been one run-in after another with them." And Orion was getting pretty tired of it. What was it going to take to bring these people in?

"It's possible. Mostly he spends his days driving his truck, hunting, and drinking with his crew. He's got a few misdemeanors, but nothing like this until yesterday. My guess is he fled the area and will lay low."

"What about the flowers? Or the knife?" Tori wrapped both hands around her mug but didn't drink it.

"No prints to be found. No one saw anything around your apartment. Nothing the local florist knows. The flowers didn't come from her shop. Which makes me think that the real culprit is a lot smarter than Wayne. He's no mastermind. Just desperate for money since he's got a gambling problem."

"And Razor? Any hint of him around?" Orion tried to keep the accusation out of his tone, but this was getting ridiculous. Copper Mountain was a small town, and they couldn't find any witnesses? "Have you found anything?"

The sheriff stared him down. "This is a big county with a lot of wilderness to cover. Why do you think people like Razor come here to disappear? We are looking. We're not going to back down."

"I appreciate that." Tori stood. "If there's nothing else, I've got a lot of dishes to wash."

"I'm sorry I don't have more, but this isn't finished yet. Be careful, and whatever you do, I suggest you don't go anywhere alone." The sheriff left.

Tori grabbed a half-empty plate and scraped the food into the big trash can. Her hand shook.

"Hey." Orion took the plate from her, set it on the counter. He wrapped her in his arms. "We're gonna get this guy. We will."

She snuggled into his chest. "I know."

Because he might not be able to fight a fire right now, but he would keep her safe if it was the last thing he did.

Tori spun the tracker ring on her finger—a

brand new one Jade had given her—as the new airplane lifted them higher into the sky. She couldn't catch a break.

Here she was, living the dream, accomplishing what she'd set out to do, and her life was still a mess. And poor Orion was the one paying the price. Even with all his own stuff, he was looking out for her, like the way he'd calmed her last night after the sheriff had left.

She looked across the aisle to where Hammer sat with his head leaning against the seat back. Eyes closed, completely at ease. Just a guy covering an open spot as a smokejumper so they'd have an even number.

It should be Orion there.

She shouldn't hold it against Hammer that it wasn't.

Not that she couldn't do this just fine without Orion. But it didn't feel right taking off to fight this fire without him.

And he wasn't taking it well. The others may not have noticed that tightening of his lips when they were called out. The way he'd waved them on as he sat at one of the sewing machines, repairing a chute like he was too busy to look up. But she'd caught that clench in his jaw as they left.

He'd fought so hard to be on this team. It

had to be torturing him to be stuck back at base camp, patching up parachutes and mowing the lawn around the base, which she knew was next on the list Tucker had given him. All because he'd saved her and messed up his shoulder. She was costing him his dream.

Logan, Skye, Cadee, and Vince all joked around.

Jade leaned closer to her. "You okay?"

"Why wouldn't I be?"

"It's been a crazy couple of weeks. You've been shot at, almost abducted. But you need to put all that aside now and get your head in the game." Jade's eyes seemed to bore into her.

"I promise you, I'm good." She threw her boss a grin that hopefully looked more convincing than it felt.

"Hammer is good too. I know you're not used to jumping with him, but I wouldn't have brought him on if I had any doubts."

"I know." Tori cinched her strap to tighten the reserve chute resting on her chest, ready to be done with this conversation.

"All right, everyone. Final checks. Let's be ready." Jade addressed the group, practically yelling to be heard over the roar of the engines.

"Logan, you're going first. Then Tori and on down the line."

When they reached height, the spotter opened the hatch, and Logan sat in the doorway, his feet dangling out in the air, his yellow static line hooked in. Tori waited behind him, taking in the landscape. Smoke rose from a stand of trees, an orange glow running along the ground. She spotted the drop zone and nearest water source. If need be, they could make it to the small lake over to the east. But the fire didn't look too bad. Not yet.

Their spotter, Mark, clapped Logan on the back and sent him off. Tori quickly followed. The last time she'd jumped, she'd snagged a tree. That wasn't going to happen today.

She spun as she fell, wind coming through her mesh face mask, almost taking her breath away with the first rush of adrenaline.

Whoosh.

Her chute opened and silence reigned. This was the part she loved. Hovering between heaven and earth. A new sense of awe bubbled inside.

Lord, You are amazing. Protect us.

And be with Orion too.

Tori relished the moments in the air. As soon as she set down, it was time to work. She gathered her chute and helped Logan unpack the equipment. Once the others joined them, they set up a temporary camp and got to work.

Tori and Cadee worked on the fire line, digging up the brush down to the mineral soil, stealing the fire's fuel.

"That was a nice landing," Cadee said. "You'd never know it's your first year."

"Thanks." Tori broke up the ground with the grub hoe end of her Pulaski.

Cadee glanced over. "You okay?"

"I feel bad for Orion. He should be here." And yes, part of it was that she *wanted* him here. He was sweet and safe in the best of ways.

Which made him more dangerous than jumping out of airplanes and fighting fires.

"You two seem to have gotten a lot closer. Not that it's surprising, especially with all you went through."

Tori paused. "He has a way of growing on a person."

Cadee laughed. "Oh, it's so much more than that. The boy is *fine*. And he seems to care about you. A lot."

"Maybe, but I'm not sure he should. I have a horrible track record with men."

"That's why the sheriff had to talk to you? Something about an ex?"

"Apparently someone wants to make my life miserable. Chances are it's my ex. Probably hired that jerk at the saloon to drug and kidnap me. He'd have easy access to drugs."

"One bad ex doesn't mean you shouldn't pursue something with Orion now. We already know he's one of the good ones."

"If only it were one bad ex. But it's like I attract the worst. Even at the Refuge, Jeremiah cornered me and thought he could do whatever he wanted. And I'm sick of guys like that. I don't really need a man in my life. Especially now that . . ."

"What?" Cadee stopped digging and looked at her.

"It's all kinda new, but . . . I have God now. I pushed Him away for so long, convinced trusting Him made me weak. But I know what the people at the Refuge were talking about. The saving grace. And I don't want to give Him up."

"You don't have to give up your faith for a relationship. A good relationship, whether that's with Orion or anyone else, should help you grow in your faith, encourage you and challenge you. If Orion shares your faith, why not move forward?"

Good question. But the answer bubbled up to the surface and was out of her mouth before she could stop it. "Maybe I don't trust myself. Not after the stupid stuff I did with guys in school or Razor. Orion deserves better." The guy hadn't even danced before the night they met. He was wholesome and . . . good.

And she most definitely wasn't.

She came with baggage. And a stalker. Orion was already grounded and missing out on fulfilling his legacy because he'd saved her and tried to take Wayne Osborne down. Basically because of her.

"I don't think you understand grace quite yet. You're God's child, Tori. He lavishes love on you. He's not disappointed in you, and this stalker is not something you deserve. It's evil and darkness. But God's grace will prevail."

Through many dangers, toils, and snares,
I have already come:
'Tis grace has brought me safe thus far,
And grace will lead me home.

"Maybe. But I don't want Orion to have to pay the price for my bad choices."

"Love bears all and keeps no record of wrongs. That's from 1 Corinthians 13. If it's the real deal with Orion, you'll know, Tori. At least give him a chance."

"I'll think about it."

She was already attached, wishing he were here.

And yet, she didn't want him to get hurt because of her. And until they could find Razor, there was a good chance her past would continue to remind her why she was better off alone.

ELEVEN

ORION PARKED THE BASE TRUCK AND stared up at the hardware store sign. He should be out there fighting the fire with his crew. Not shopping for lawn mower parts. He was now relegated to groundskeeper, tasked to mow the grass around the jump base. His shoulder hurt, but it wasn't debilitating. He'd be fine if they would let him jump.

But nope. He was grounded.

He'd done everything right. He'd sacrificed. Pushed hard. He'd even waited to take this shot until his mother was ready. So why had God sidelined him now?

But he wouldn't be for long. He just had to get through today. Tomorrow, Jade was going to test him. If he was healed enough, he'd be back on the crew.

His phone rang as he stepped out of the truck. *Dad.*

Still weird to see that word pop up on a screen.

Up until last year, he hadn't known who his father was. But when Charlie Benning had shown up last year to join the Jude County Hotshots, it'd been obvious he had a history with Jayne Price. It hadn't taken long to connect the dots and realize he was Orion's father and that Jayne had never told him she was pregnant. They'd come a long way in the last year.

"Hey, is everything okay?" Orion answered.

Charlie Benning chuckled. "I was gonna ask you the same thing. All good here. But we hadn't heard from you in a while. And Jade reached out."

"My boss is calling my parents? Why do I feel like a kid in trouble at school?" And if he sounded grumpy, so be it. This was ridiculous.

"Don't get your shorts tied up in a knot. It wasn't like that. She called a few days ago to see if we had any connections to get an airplane, but when I casually asked how you were doing, she was surprised we hadn't heard from you ourselves. Said there was a lot going on, but she wouldn't say anything more. Your mom and I waited a few more days, and when we still didn't hear anything, I thought I'd reach out. I know you're busy, Ry, but we've been concerned."

"You don't need to worry about an airplane. Logan's girlfriend Jamie is loaded. She bought a new Twin Otter for the base camp."

"That's not what we're worried about. But why'd she do that?"

"Probably her way of thanking us for rescuing her and her brother Tristan from this militia they got caught up in."

"Yeah, but a new plane? What was wrong with the one the team was already using? It need an upgrade?"

There was a reason he hadn't been in touch. But guess there was no going back now. "Um, it crashed."

His father was silent for a moment. "I'm assuming no one was in it when it went down?"

Orion winced. "Only Neil and Saxon, but they're okay now. The rest of us jumped before it hit the ground. Which is why I didn't say anything. No need to worry Mom. I know she has a hard time with me being out here in the first place."

"She's come to terms with you being a smoke-jumper. But she's not happy about you ghosting us. I get you wanted a fresh start, but we didn't think that meant you'd cut off all communication."

"I wasn't trying to. It's just been busy, and Tori and I got waylaid on our way back to base. And I thought you understood that when I moved out here, things would be different. I have to do this on my own."

"That's why you went out to Alaska instead of staying with the Jude County crew here?"

Orion gripped the phone. "I didn't want any favors. I needed to know that I didn't make the team because of who my parents are or who my grandfather was."

And maybe also, come to think of it, because if he failed, he wouldn't have to face the disappointment in his mother's eyes again. And now his father's too.

And yet word had still gotten back to them, thanks to Jade.

Apparently, Alaska wasn't far enough.

"What are you trying to prove, Orion?" Charlie's voice came through strong, steady. The question probed at the dark places inside though.

But his dad had only come into his life last year. He hadn't been there. He didn't understand.

"Mom sacrificed everything to raise me. Her

own mother kicked her out of the house because of me. Now it's time for me to do this. To show Mom that—" He couldn't finish the sentence.

"That it wasn't a waste?"

How did he do that? Read his mind even though they'd only met a year ago.

"Maybe." Orion kicked at a pebble. "I have a legacy to live up to. Grandpa Jack. Mom. You. I want my life to mean something."

"I get that. But the legacy that is most worth achieving is a life surrendered to God. It's not all up to you. And it doesn't mean you have to push everyone else away to do that. Come on, kid. You barely escaped a plane crash and didn't tell us? Is there anything else that happened?"

Orion pushed the hair off his forehead and grabbed his neck. "I . . . may have injured my shoulder and hit my head pretty good while we were running away from the militia, but that was a couple weeks ago."

"I see." Charlie paused. "But . . . you're okay now? The jumps are going okay?"

"I'm not jumping right now."

"Why not?"

So he was going to make him spill the whole humiliating story? Fine. "Tori—my partner—and I were separated from the group when we jumped.

We were stuck on this commune for a couple days, and now we're back. But Tori has a stalker. Someone tried to abduct her, and in fighting him off, I reinjured my shoulder. I'm grounded. So ... Mom's probably glad about that."

"Glad? Not hardly! Don't you get it? We're here for you. Praying for you every day. Why wouldn't you tell us what you're going through?"

Orion winced. "I don't want you to worry. I've got this. Sure, it sucks to be grounded, but I'm fine."

"We know it's a dangerous job, but that's why there's a team. It's not a solo gig. And as your family, we're part of your team too. You guys taught me that last year. I was ready to face my kidney disease alone, thinking Alexa, and then your mom and you and everyone on God's green earth, was better off without me. But there is strength in relying on others. And here I am in remission. Because you guys wouldn't let me do this alone. So I'm gonna push back. You don't have to do this alone either, Ry."

Didn't he? Wasn't that part of being a man and standing on his own two feet? But it was nice to know Charlie cared. That his mom and sister were there for him too. "I'll try to do better at keeping you in the loop. Jade is going to run me through some drills, and if I pass them, I'll be back on the crew. But you're not gonna fly out here with a cheer section or anything, are you?"

"No promises. I'm sure I can find a set of pom-poms and a flight to Anchorage in a pinch."

Orion cracked a smile. "As long as I don't have to see you in a skirt."

"Deal." Charlie paused. "So, you mentioned your partner. Tori? Is she okay? What's going on with this stalker business?"

"She's strong, good. Even better than she was before, since she's come to faith through the whole situation. But this creep is still out there, and there's a lot going on. I'm doing everything I can to protect her."

"And is there anything... more to this relationship with Tori? She sounds like a special woman."

"She is. And I guess the short answer is... I'm not sure. I like her. A lot. We were rivals for a bit, but I dunno. Things have shifted."

"A believer. A strong woman. And she doesn't mind your company? Sounds like something to pray about."

"Sure. Add it to the list."

"I will. But I better let you go. Before I do, I think your mom would appreciate a call. I'll leave it at that. She's out with the wilderness kids on an overnight though."

"Tell her I'll call her tomorrow." Orion sighed. "Thanks, Dad."

"Anytime, kid."

They said their goodbyes and hung up. Best get back to what he'd come here for.

Orion pushed open the door to the hardware store, the smell of lumber welcoming him. A few other people lingered in the store. After finding the lawn mower blades, he asked the woman at the counter where to find mulch.

"You purchase it here at the counter and then drive around back. We'll get ya loaded up in the lumber yard."

Orion ordered what he needed and drove the truck around the block to the back of the store. He scoped out the mulch, but everything in reaching distance was gone. They'd need a lift to get the unopened pallet on the top shelf.

Noise came from the other side of the shelving.

"Hello?" Orion called as he moved to the next aisle. Nothing. "I could use some help. Anybody there?"

Suddenly a tower of packaged cedar shavings toppled over, knocking him to the ground.

And trapping him.

Orion sucked in a breath and yelled, "Someone help!"

Tori beat the low flames with her wet burlap. It wasn't glamorous work, but she loved it. There was something therapeutic about smothering fire and stomping out the destructive nature of it. Funny that once it'd been darkness she'd fought.

Now she was fighting a source of light.

But unlike the sun that gave good light and provided warmth, not asking anything of people, fire didn't play fair. It burned and left ash and darkness behind. It was selfish and all-consuming, its light deceiving, drawing her in only to burn her, destroying whatever was in its path. And here she was fighting back.

Take that!

She smothered the orange embers at her feet, the grass now black and ashen.

She walked back over to the tank they'd set up and wet the burlap again.

"Hanging in there?" Jade asked as she mopped her face with a dripping wet bandanna.

"All good."

"I think we've almost got this one. It's creeping, and with the night shift coming in, they'll probably be able to finish it off. There's another crew out of Fairbanks fighting a smaller blaze just north of here too. So we're gonna gather up and pack out. Buses are waiting for us three miles out. Go ahead and gather your gear."

"Got it."

The packs were heavy, some weighing as much as she did, but the guys were good about taking the heavier ones. She hefted her load and marched with Cadee and JoJo.

"I'm beat." JoJo munched on a granola bar.

"Packouts after a grueling day of beating out fires are just cruel." Cadee made a face.

Tori grinned.

"What are you smiling about?" JoJo asked her.

"Nothing. I guess after being out of the game for a while, I'm glad to be here, even if it's sweaty and tiring work."

"Or"—Cadee stopped and adjusted her load—"you're excited to see Orion and now have something to look forward to beyond a hot shower and decent meal."

"Maybe." Why bother denying it? "I hope he's all right."

"*I* hope he made us something delicious for dinner. I could eat an elephant." JoJo pocketed her wrapper and marched on.

After hiking three miles, then a long bus ride, it was good to see the Midnight Sun Wildland Firefighting crew sign.

When they pulled up to the equipment hangar, they unloaded gear. Tori glanced around as she dropped off her chute. No sign of Orion.

Walking over to the women's cabin, she continued to look for him. The grassy areas surrounding the buildings and hangars hadn't been mowed.

It wasn't like Orion to shirk a duty like that. Tori tried to shake off the dread growing as she showered and changed. Something must've come up. She didn't bother with a hair dryer, just slipped her stocking feet into her Birkies and headed to the mess hall.

Orion stood in the kitchen, his arm in a sling again. He was talking to Logan, who hefted a big pot of sloppy joe mix to the serving counter. Orion brought bags of buns in his good hand.

"What happened?" Tori took the bags from him.

"A mishap at the hardware store. I dislocated the shoulder this time."

"But how?"

"Not sure, but I think someone is out to get me. You know those big bales of cedar shavings? A tower of them suspiciously toppled and knocked me over. I tripped over a pile of bird seed and landed on the same shoulder. It's not as bad as it looks. It popped back in on its own."

Like that made it better? Tori bit down hard, ready to pummel someone.

"You think it was on purpose?" Logan asked.

"Someone was there. They wouldn't show themselves, but I heard them. The store doesn't have cameras, so I don't have proof." Orion grabbed a serving spoon and jabbed a chunk of meat in the pot. "Doctor thinks I'll need surgery, but I'm gonna put it off until the season is done."

"You can't possibly be thinking of fighting fires like this." Logan nodded at the arm in a sling.

"Why not? This is why I'm here. We're not even halfway through the season. A couple weeks, and I'll be good enough to jump."

Would he? This was the third time he'd injured his shoulder.

And who would want to hurt Orion? It had to be connected to her. Razor must've seen her out with Orion. He was always the jealous type.

And this was why she shouldn't start anything with Orion Price. His last name said it all. He would pay for her mistakes.

The rest of the crew came in a group, rowdy

and hungry. Tori waited her turn in line and sat between Cadee and JoJo at one of the tables.

"What happened to Orion?" JoJo asked.

Tori told her and promptly bit into her sloppy joe.

"Why aren't you with him? Don't you want to help nurse him back to health?" Cadee waggled her eyebrows.

Considering it was her fault he was in this situation to begin with, she was probably the last person Orion would want to be around.

Tori quickly changed the subject. Orion and Vince joined them at the table with their plates.

"How was the fire?" Probably Orion wanted to steer the conversation away from his injury. She would've.

"This one wasn't bad. It wasn't out completely, but the night shift will hopefully wrap it up."

After the meal, the crew broke off into pairs and smaller groups. Tori scraped her plate and left the mess hall.

Orion was waiting for her outside. "Hey, are you okay?"

"Of course." She glanced over at him as they walked across the runway to the firepit.

"You don't seem okay. Did something happen while you were at the fire site?"

"Yeah. You got hurt." She stopped, jammed her hands into the pocket of her sweatshirt.

"So you're pushing me away now? Why?"

"Orion, do you really not know? Look at what happens to you!" She gestured to his sling.

"Hey." He grabbed one of her hands and faced her. "None of this is your fault."

Wasn't it? "If it weren't for me, you would be doing what you came here to do. Smokejumping. And . . ."

The wind kicked up, a stiff breeze blowing long blonde strands—now dried—across her face.

"And what?" His voice was soft, but the concern in it was strong. "Tori, please don't shut me out. Right now . . . you're the only thing going right in my life."

"Me?" How was that possible?

"Yeah, you." He tugged her closer, let go of her hand, and moved the hair out of her eyes. Cupped her chin. "You're all I've been able to think about."

She stepped closer, wrapped her fingers into the fabric of his fleece. She should push him away, but his gaze drew her in. "I hated going out there without you. But . . . I'm scared, Ry."

"I'm not going to hurt you, Tori. I'm not like Razor or Wayne Osborne or any of those guys."

"I know. I do, but . . ." She glanced down at the

212

cross he wore on a chain. "What if I hurt you? I have a tendency to make bad choices with men. And this time it's not the guy who is the bad choice. The common denominator in all those relationships was me. What if I screw this up too? What if you're too good for someone like me?"

"Someone like you? If only I could be so lucky." The tender note of his voice brought her gaze back to his eyes. They were bright and clear, focused solely on her. A slight blush swept across his strong cheekbones. "I haven't been able to escape you from the first night we met. I don't want to. You have this light in you that glows, Tori. You're strong and brave and care about others. What's not to love?"

Love? Her breath caught.

Had he really said love?

He didn't backpedal. His eyes stayed on hers. His Adam's apple bobbed as he swallowed, waiting.

And she didn't want to wait any longer.

Tori pulled him in and kissed him. And this time she didn't hold back. Their lips met with fire and heat. Her fingers slid around his neck and tangled up in his hair. He tightened his hold around her waist, bringing her closer. Safer. Kissing him was like skydiving—for a moment, the heart-stopping drop, a little trepidation, and then . . . sheer wonder as the chute opened and caught the wind. She was flying. And she didn't want to land.

Orion forged a trail of gentle kisses from her mouth, along her jaw, and up to her ear, where he whispered, "Victoria, I think I'm falling for you."

She pulled back a moment, looking into his beautiful blue eyes. "Good."

Because in this moment, she knew. She was too far gone now, and maybe this time it was okay since she'd finally picked the right kind of guy.

A hero.

TWELVE

THE NEXT MORNING AT THE DEBRIEF, Tucker pulled up the area map. Orion stood at the back of the room, trying not to brood or grumble. He was there only to be close to Tori since he was pretty much useless physically. It would be another day of mowing lawn and repairing equipment for him.

But he had Tori's kiss from last night to keep him company. He'd lost all sense of time with her. But she was the one thing that made sense right now. He couldn't understand why God had brought him to Alaska only to be injured.

And now it was more than just not being able to live up to his calling, to be redeemed from his past mistakes. How was he supposed to watch Tori's back if they got called out?

Tucker started the meeting. "Unfortunately, the wind last night whipped up the fire we almost had under control yesterday. It merged with another fire, and now we have a problem on our hands." He pointed to the expansive forested area.

Great. They would be jumping today. Without him.

"What direction is the wind blowing?" Tori asked.

"Coming from the northwest. It's pushing this thing right up the mountain to the east."

Orion pushed off the wall. "That fire is headed straight for the Refuge."

"Which is why we're deploying ASAP. Everyone get your gear." Jade checked her watch. "Plane's going up in twenty. Hotshot bus will be leaving sooner."

The rest of the crews headed out, leaving Orion behind . . . except Tori. She looked back at him, her expression asking, *What do we do?*

He moved to the front of the room and approached Tucker Newman. "I know I can't fight the fire, but I can help on the ground at the Refuge. They'll be reluctant to leave."

"I know." Tucker turned off the screen he'd used

to display the map. "Last night's crew reached out to the Brinks and asked them to get a message over. They got back to us this morning. The residents of the Refuge won't budge."

Tori stood shoulder to shoulder with Orion. "We know this group. We were there with them. Send us in."

Tucker shook his head. "We need you on the line. And you"—he pointed at Orion—"shouldn't be going anywhere. In a couple days we might consider putting you on the plane as a spotter, but for now—"

"For now, this is how I can be useful. Send me in."

"With everything that's going on, I'm not sending anyone out there alone."

"I'll go with him," Tori said. "You have two Trouble Boys who can jump. Have either Saxon or Hammer take my place. Orion and I already have a rapport with the group. They're slow to trust outsiders. If they'll listen to anyone, it will be us."

Tucker looked at Jade and Mitch. "You two okay with this plan?"

They both nodded.

"Okay." He stood, hands on his hips, and stared them down. "Pack what you need. Take one of the trucks, keep your radios and a backup sat phone close. You stay in communication. That's imperative. Got it?"

"Yes, sir," Orion and Tori said in unison.

"Get those people out of there. This fire is growing by the minute." Tucker turned to leave.

Finally, Orion could be useful again. It took longer than he liked packing one-handed, but they grabbed chain saws, fuel, and tools—everything they could find to help fight a fire—and threw it in the back of the white truck with the Midnight Sun logo on the doors.

"We'll need more than a truck if we have to evacuate the group." Tori's words stopped him. She looked at him over the bed of the truck. "There's, like, forty people out there."

She was right. "We need a fleet of vehicles. Maybe the Brinks will help us."

"It's still not enough. They have their family and probably animals they'll be evacuating."

"I did see some four-wheelers in their shed, but it won't be enough." Orion set another Pulaski in the truck bed.

"Or . . . I can drive one of the base-camp buses. I mean, not legally, but I know how."

"Even on that low-maintenance road to the Brinks' homestead? It's pretty rough."

"We have to get them to safety." With that

stubborn tilt to her chin, she probably wasn't going to back down.

"All right. Do it. I'll follow you in the truck."

"You okay to drive one-handed?"

He walked around the cab of the truck and kissed her. "I'll be fine. Let's go save some people."

She smiled up at him. "Okay."

Tori ignored the posted speed limit on the paved road, which was fine with this Montana boy who took full advantage of the 80mph on the interstate back home. They had people to save. But it was called backcountry for a reason. Their base camp was already on the edge of civilization.

Out here it was all wide open sky, trees and meadows, and mountain giants looming in the distance. They passed vehicles on the highway, but once they turned off the main drag, the roads were rough. And no wonder. They were cut out of the wilderness, which wanted to reclaim the territory. Trees encroached on both sides.

The top of the bus brushed against branches. Orion bounced as his truck hit pothole after pothole. At this rate, he might injure his rear along with the shoulder. But he pushed the pain aside. Eventually, they reached the end of the road. The Brinks' homestead.

They pulled up to Kitri strapping down a cage

of chickens in the back of a truck. "I didn't expect to see you two again so soon." She walked over to them. A man with red hair and a barrel chest joined her.

"This is my husband, Cameron. These are the two that brought me to Copper Mountain."

Cameron shook their hands. "Thank you for helping my wife. What can we do for you?"

"We came to help evacuate the people at the Refuge," Tori said.

Cameron raised an eyebrow. "Good luck with that. They're good people, but they're stubborn. They won't leave. I spent all morning trying to talk some sense into them."

A teenage boy in jeans and a sweatshirt carried a goat to the truck. Kitri opened the tailgate for him. "Thanks, Kyle." She turned to the group. "We've got more animals to load."

Cameron nodded. "You're welcome to use what you can find, but Kitri's right. We've still got more to do, and this smoke is getting bad."

"How close do you get to the Refuge on that path with a vehicle?" Orion asked.

"You'll never get that bus down there; you'll have to leave it here. But you can get an ATV with a little trailer that I use. You'll find it in the shed over there. Keys are in it." He pointed to a gray metal-sided building by the barn. "The truck will probably get stuck but might be worth the risk to see how far you can get it."

Orion and Tori thanked them. A few more kids—a girl with long brown braids like her mom, and two more boys—loaded bags in the back of their vehicle and barely glanced at their parents.

"Can you drive the ATV?" Orion asked Tori. "I think I might try to get the truck as close as I can."

"Let's do it."

The Brink family left in two vehicles as Tori hit the trail on the ATV in the opposite direction. Orion followed her in the truck. At least the trail was dry. But it was tight. Branches and brush scraped the windows and sides of the truck. How he would get out of here, he'd try to figure out later.

Tori made a sharp turn around a patch of white spruce.

Yeah, the truck wouldn't make that. And there wasn't enough room in any direction to go off-trail.

He honked and killed the engine. Tori stopped the ATV.

"This is the end of the road for the truck."

"You made it about halfway at least." She lifted a couple of Pulaskis and shovels from the truck bed and added them to the open trailer behind the ATV.

They loaded chain saws and everything they could and took off. Tori drove. Orion didn't mind at all holding on to her as they continued through the dense forest.

They drove until the forest cleared, back to the commune. Through the smoky haze, the chapel and dining hall stood guard over the sides of the community, with cabins flanking the wide grassy area in the middle. If it weren't for the smoke clogging the air, he would've seen the river peeking through the trees. Amos and Hannah stood on the chapel steps, talking and watching over everyone. Except for a few curious glances, everyone moved quickly. Mara stopped when she caught sight of them.

"Orion! Victoria!" She rushed over. "What are you doing here?"

"Didn't expect to see you two back here." Amos walked up to them and met them in the middle of the lawn.

"There's a big fire headed here. We came to warn you." Orion offered Tori a hand off the ATV.

"Like I told Cameron Brink, we appreciate the warning, but we won't be leaving our home."

Orion wanted to shake the man. "Amos, you're

putting your people at risk. We have a bus and can get you all to safety. You can rebuild the structures. You can't replace lives."

"True. And I inquired of the Lord when we heard about the fire. We're staying."

"You can't be serious." Tori folded her arms across her chest.

"I'm always serious. And if you two don't mind, we're making preparations, and you're keeping me from my work. If you want to help, by all means help." Amos started to walk away.

"What are you doing to prepare?" Orion followed the man.

"We're hauling river water and wetting down all the buildings we can, bringing the animals in." He pointed to three men hauling up a canoe filled with water. They grabbed buckets and scooped the water out of it, splashing it around the first cabin.

"That's not enough. We need a fire line. We need to remove the fuel that feeds the fire, create a protective boundary it won't cross around the commune. We have to clear the brush and trees, get down to the mineral soil. You might have a chance if you do that, but with the timeline we have, it's slim."

Amos stopped and actually smiled at Orion. "See, I knew the Lord would provide."

There was no way the Refuge would survive this fire without help.

Tori called into base camp. "We need equipment and people. They won't leave."

Smoke already hung in the air, and ash rained down like snow.

"The crew is already out fighting the fire at the flank, trying to redirect it. We can drop some equipment, maybe some water on the structures. But there isn't anyone else here and no way to get to you." Tucker's voice crackled over the radio.

Tori released a short breath. It wasn't enough. "We'll take what we can get."

"I'll let you know when we're ready for the drop."

Tori walked over to Orion, who was handing out tools to a line of men, teenagers, and young girls. "They'll drop some water to help save the structures, some equipment too, but everyone is out fighting the fire. There's no one left to help."

He nodded. "We'll get started on the line on the west side. The river to the north will hopefully protect that side. Can you show the women how to use the flamethrower and burn any underbrush around the structures? We have burlap we can use too when that time comes."

"I'll teach them that, but then I'm coming back here. You can't operate a chain saw with your shoulder in a sling."

"I'll use the Pulaski one-handed." He shrugged like it was no big deal.

But Tori didn't like this. She quickly showed Mara, Joann—who carried Josiah in a baby sling—and Gabby the flamethrower and gave them a shovel and burlap to put out any little fires that might get out of hand.

Hannah watched and listened. When Tori was finished explaining, Hannah pointed to her finger. "Why aren't you wearing your ring?"

Shoot. Tori had forgotten to put her tracker ring on before leaving. "I think we have more important things to worry about, like keeping everyone safe."

Hannah's lips thinned. "I'll take another group of girls if you have another flamethrower. We can start on the other end."

Tori showed her the tools in the trailer and left. She hiked out to the west of the commune, where the men were already at work cutting down trees and clearing a line.

"Can I come with you?" Gabby skipped behind her. "The other ladies can do the burning."

"It's dangerous, kiddo. And heavy work. You'll be dragging big branches and—"

"I can do that. And I won't complain. At all."

She was so eager to help. And hey, maybe her energy and enthusiasm would be a boost. Tori couldn't think about the chances of them actually pulling off the fire line in time. Not at the rate the fire was moving.

"All right. Come with me."

Orion hadn't been lying about what he could accomplish with one good arm. He'd gripped his Pulaski in his right hand and was quickly breaking up the soil. One of the little boys came after him with a raking tool and cleared out vegetation. Abraham and another man worked on felling trees and limbs. One group moved north toward the river. Orion's group extended the line south. They'd probably curve east eventually. Tori directed Gabby and some of the older girls on how to drag away the branches before she grabbed another chain saw.

Lord, please protect us.

She joined Orion's crew and started mowing down limbs, stealing fuel from the raging monster on its way. Sweat and ash covered their faces, sawdust flecked their hair. Though the muscles in her arm screamed at the exertion, she pressed on. She had to hand it to the group. They worked hard. And they needed to. Everyone in this community depended on it.

The smoke thickened. Some of the younger children brought water for them and handkerchiefs to tie around their noses and mouths.

But they didn't let up. They couldn't. The fire certainly wouldn't.

And it was coming. By now they could hear the crackle and dull roar.

Orion stopped a moment and pushed the damp hair off his forehead. "This is bad. Don't know if it will be enough." He sucked in a few deep breaths.

Her arms were shaking as she set down the chain saw. "We need the aerial support. I'll check on it."

Tori called in. "Midnight Sun, this is Tori. What's the ETA on that water drop?"

The voice on the other side of the radio came through. "The scooper is grabbing water right now. They're on their way."

"Drop it on the structures. We're going to need all the protection we can get."

"ETA is seven minutes."

"We'll be ready."

Orion sent word up the line. "We won't be hit with the water here, but we need to make sure everyone in the area knows."

Tori turned to Gabby. "Go make sure everyone back at the commune is inside a building until the water drops. Then they can go back to whatever they were doing. Run!"

The girl threw down the branch she'd been dragging and took off.

Amos walked over to them, his face flushed, hair matted down, wet with perspiration.

Orion told him about the drop. "We still have a chance to evacuate, but that window is closing fast. If we can get everyone to the Brinks', there's a bus—"

"I already told you," Amos said as he shook his head, "we're staying. The Lord will protect us."

"How can you be so sure?" Tori asked him.

"He brought you." Amos turned and went back to where one of the other men had cut down a small spruce. Amos dragged it over the fire line.

Orion looked at Tori. "We better get the line finished."

The sound of an engine broke through the din of chain saws.

Finally.

Everyone on the line stopped and looked up. Within seconds, a cool mist rained down on them, the majority of the water hitting the commune just as they'd requested. Orion grinned at Tori. The air felt clearer, the water dispelling some of the smoke. Hopefully, it soaked the buildings enough to protect them from flying sparks.

They might have a chance at this.

Gabby ran back, sopping wet and laughing. "That was fun!" Her smile was infectious.

"Everyone okay?" Tori asked her.

She nodded and grabbed another branch to move.

The whine of another engine broke through the trees as Tori bent down to pick up her chain saw.

"Is the airplane coming back?" Gabby paused.

"Not this soon." More engines sounded. From slightly different directions.

A gunshot went off.

Orion dropped his Pulaski and rushed up the slight incline to the west. He pulled out a small pair of field binoculars and scouted the area.

He suddenly spun around and yelled to Tori, "Get the girls and run!"

"What is it?" She wasn't going anywhere until she knew what threat was coming.

He sprinted back to her, a stormy look in his eyes she only saw when he was facing down people like Wayne Osborne. "You'll never believe—" He grunted and snatched his Pulaski up, not bothering to finish his statement. "We have to go!" he shouted to the others in the line and waved them toward the commune.

"Ry, what's going on? Who is it?" Tori stopped him.

He dropped his voice low. "Who do you know with a fleet of ATVs and guns?"

Tori's breath caught. "You don't think—"

"Yes, I do. Get those girls out of here. The militia is back!"

THIRTEEN

ORION HAD TO FORGET THE FIRE line and get these people to safety. Just when he was beginning to feel like they were going to be okay with a raging wildland fire headed straight toward them, now he had the militia invading. With his Pulaski in hand, Orion jogged up the line to the other men. "Go back to the commune!"

The men and boys stopped and looked at him. With wet hair and faces covered in dirt and ash, they blended in with the trees. But it wasn't nearly enough camouflage to hide from the militia.

"What's going on?" Amos walked over. Abraham was right behind him.

"There's a militia group on their way right

now. I don't know what they want, but it won't be good. You need to get everyone out of here."

"And leave you to face it all?" Amos glared. "We face the threat together. Like the fire."

"These guys have guns. They're not friendly. Go back and protect the women and children. You can leave—"

"We're not leaving the Refuge. I already told you that." Amos didn't look like he would budge.

One of the engines revved. They were getting closer. Abraham looked back toward the commune. "But he's right. We shouldn't leave the women and children defenseless."

"I'll do what I can to hold them off. Try to talk to them and figure out what they want. But you might need to fight. Find anything you can to arm yourselves." Orion spoke to the group, but Amos's mouth remained tight. "These are your people, your family, Amos. Go watch over them."

"We're a body for a reason. We don't fight alone."

Oh, he was a stubborn man. He'd have to be to survive in the wilds of Alaska off-grid.

But Orion could be just as determined. "I'm not alone, am I? God is my rock and my refuge."

"Amos, the children." Abraham stepped up to the leader.

Without a spoken word—but with plenty of displeasure in his expression—Amos left. The rest of the men followed, holding the tools they'd been using to fight a fire, now for a different purpose.

With that settled, Orion could focus on facing the militia.

He removed his sling. Why advertise the fact that he was wounded? He hiked the incline again. How close were they? The ATVs were moving in, the engines louder. Reaching the top of the hill, Orion stayed behind a thick spruce trunk. Three ATVs, each with two men riding, splashed in the shallows of the river, heading straight to the commune, but from the sound of it, more were coming from different directions.

What could they even want with a peaceful commune like the Refuge?

Could really use Your help here, Lord.

Amos's words came back to him.

We're a body for a reason. We don't fight alone.

He really couldn't fight them all off by himself. But he had to know the rest of the commune was safe and scope out the threat.

The smoke in the air hung heavy, obscuring his view. The fire roared close now, coming straight from the west. But the militiamen rode in from the north.

Six men, all armed and wearing various patterns of camouflage. Wait—Orion squeezed the handle of the Pulaski. That was Wayne Osborne!

They were heading straight to the village.

Where Tori was.

Forget trying to talk sense with these people. Orion spun and sprinted. He had to get to Tori, keep her safe. Hidden.

He cut around the trees and underbrush, arm in front of his face to block the branches.

"Hey! There he is!" one of the men shouted from a four-wheeler.

Orion probably sounded like a bull charging through, but at this point, he only cared about getting to Tori. He had to keep her safe. With all the trees, their ATVs would have to go the long way around by the river. He charged up the hill to cut across, his feet eating up the distance. He could see the fire line they had finished breaking. He was close. But so were the shouts from the militiamen. Sounded like a couple of them were following him on foot now. Orion slowed to slip between two smaller trees.

Something jerked around his ankle, tripping him. He hit the ground, knocking the breath out of himself.

What? His foot was caught. Orion tried to

breathe and sit up. Around his boot was thin cable. A snare.

He tried to free himself, grasping at the locking mechanism.

"Well, look what we caught, Wayne. And I didn't even have to bait the trap." A man with a dark beard, a mustache, and a mean glare stood over Orion, a rifle in hand. His sneer showed off tobacco-stained teeth.

"Guess it's our lucky day, Vlad." Wayne chuckled as he stomped up. "Where's the other one? The pretty little lady you were with."

Yeah, like he'd just give Tori up. Orion kept his mouth clamped shut. Wayne yanked him to his feet. He and Vlad each grabbed Orion's arms, a piercing pain shooting from his injured shoulder almost taking him down.

A third man hiked over. His long hair was pulled back in a grimy ponytail, and he had the longest beard of all the men. "It's about time. Now give us what we want, Trist—who is this?" He looked Orion up and down, then glared at Wayne. "Where's Tristan?"

"Ain't this him?" Wayne looked confused. "Damian said it was him, that if I took the blonde, he'd follow."

Took the blonde? Tori? That's why he'd tried to kidnap her? To bait him?

"Idiots! This isn't Tristan Winters." Ponytail Guy slapped Wayne's arm. "We've been chasing after the wrong guy!"

Tristan. Jamie Winters's brother. So that was their intended target. Sure, he and Orion both had dark hair, similar builds, and blue eyes, but . . .

"I'm not Tristan, so why don't you let me go and get out of here before the fire traps us all." He pulled against Wayne's hold since that was his uninjured side, but Wayne's grip only tightened.

"What do we do now?" Wayne asked. "Frank, you make the call."

The man with the ponytail—Frank—pulled out a knife and faced Orion. "He knows what we look like and who we're after. I say he comes with us."

Tori tried not to worry about Orion as she gathered the children into the chapel. But he was out there facing down the militia. At least he was with the other men. He had his job. She would do hers and keep these children safe.

She gathered the group of the youngest kids,

maybe seven of them together, and led the way down the center aisle between the pews.

The weak sunrays coming in through the high windows gave them dim light. But the log walls were sturdy. The little altar was nothing more than a wooden pulpit and a simple cross hanging on the wall behind it, but it was a reminder of why this group was here. And the building was the farthest east, farthest from the fire.

But what protection would it be from the militia?

Tori brought the kids to the little room behind the altar. The sounds of the ATVs seemed to be coming from everywhere all at once. One of the little girls, probably not even five, started crying. Gabby rushed over to hold her.

Tori moved to the door, back to the main part of the chapel. "Gabby, keep them here and keep them quiet. I'm going to go find Orion."

Mara and Joann rushed in with Hannah. More women followed, and Tori met them at the door.

"You all should stay here—hide if you can," Tori told them.

"Who are these people? What do they want?" Hannah stood in front of the open entrance to the chapel, ready to face down anything that tried to cross the threshold.

"It's a militia group. I don't know what they want, but it's probably my fault they're here."

"Your fault?" Mara asked.

And suddenly Tori was tired of the lies, the weight of them unbearable.

"I'm no one's answer to prayer. I brought trouble. Right to your doorstep."

"What are you talking about?" Hannah's eyes narrowed.

"Look, Orion and I aren't married. We're smokejumpers. Wildland firefighters. But one of our teammates has a friend. She was caught by this militia. We were helping rescue her and her brother when the militia shot down our airplane. Orion and I were separated from our team when we parachuted out and were injured running away from these guys. When Amos assumed we were married, we thought it was for the best that we stay together. Especially with the way Jeremiah would stare. But it looks like the militia found us again. So, I guess I'm trying to say I'm sorry."

"Why is the militia being here your fault?" Mara looked confused.

Wasn't it obvious? She attracted the worst of humanity.

"Seems to me these men are bent on destruction one way or another. That isn't your fault. As for pretending to be married, I can't say I condone lying, but under the circumstances with Jeremiah, I understand. Mara told us what happened when you left. And we haven't seen Jeremiah since." Hannah's eyes softened. "Amos and I wanted this community to be a safe place, and it wasn't for you. And for that, I'm the one that is sorry. Still . . . God works in mysterious ways. Little Josiah is thriving. You're here just in time to help us fight this fire. That's not a coincidence. I'd say you are exactly the answer to prayer we needed."

"If you don't want to marry Orion, do you think he'd marry me?" Gabby tugged on her arm, all the children that should've been hiding trailing behind her.

Tori chuckled. "We're not married, but . . . he might be the answer to the prayer I didn't even know to pray. And—"

Two ATVs sped into the middle of the commune, tearing up the grass.

"Get back!" Tori shooed the women away from the door. "Take the children into the back room—better yet, the basement." Most of the women did as she asked, except Hannah and Mara. They stayed by Tori at the doorway of the chapel.

"You're not alone, Victoria. We do this together." Hannah walked through the door.

They stood on the steps of the chapel, ready to face the four men. Maybe Tori could lure them away.

Suddenly a shout, and Amos and the other men from the fire line ran onto the open lawn. But the militia took aim with rifles and pistols.

"No!" Tori leaped off the steps and stood between the two groups of men, facing the militia. "Don't hurt these people. They've done nothing to you."

One of the men, probably the leader from the way the others watched him, got off his ATV. He was bald, a dirty green bandanna tied around his neck. "The fact that you're here says otherwise. If they've been harboring Tristan Winters—"

"Tristan? Jamie's brother? He isn't here. He never was."

"Like I'm going to take your word for it." The bald man held his rifle and walked up to her.

"You should. She tells the truth." Amos came and stood next to Tori. "We have no quarrel with you. Leave us now, before that changes."

An evil grin crept onto the militia leader's face. "You don't wanna cross me, old man."

Tori wasn't sure how it started, but a brawl

broke out as the Refuge men surged the four militiamen, wrestling away guns and knocking each other to the ground. Tori jumped out of the way while Abraham tackled one of the men. She spun to check on the women. Thick arms grabbed her from behind.

She thrashed and kicked, but the man was strong, his grip unbreakable. He dragged her away behind the structure. She opened her mouth to shout. A gloved hand clamped down, cutting off her scream.

"Not so fast. This time you won't get away." The voice in her ear was familiar. But from where?

She could hardly hear with the blood rushing to her head. A gag was stuffed into her mouth, choking her. A sharp prick in her neck, and she felt a burning liquid forced under her skin. Her body went weak.

No! She threw her head back, butting her assailant.

He roared. But he didn't stop.

He merely picked her up and threw her over his shoulder. She grabbed a tree branch as he moved away from the commune into the woods, but it slipped right through her hands. Her eyes barely stayed open. Whatever he'd shot into her was taking effect fast.

Another sound registered.

Water. He was taking her to the river.

Help me, Lord.

Help me out of this danger.

The man tossed her into one of the canoes. She blinked, looked up at his face. It blurred and then finally came into focus.

It wasn't Jeremiah or Razor or Wayne, but she knew this man's strength and determination. If only she'd realized in time that he was sick too.

"You can't ignore me now. Finally, we'll have some alone time, and you'll see how perfect we can be together, Tori."

Her eyes closed and everything faded into oblivion.

FOURTEEN

I F THE MILITIA DIDN'T KILL HIM, THE fire might.

As it was, they used the snare to cinch Orion's wrists together and marched him at gunpoint back to the commune. A glance behind him showed the fire devouring the forest, flames shooting high, sparks flying even higher. The men holding Orion kicked it into double time while three others ran for the ATVs.

"We'll drive them upriver and meet you at the commune," Vlad said.

Orion could breathe a little easier once they passed the fire line they'd broken. Hopefully it would be enough to deviate the roaring monster away from the Refuge. Still, the air was all ash and smoke. And their line was hastily done, sacrificing width to get more distance around the structures.

"We need to get to shelter." Orion had to yell over the fire to be heard.

Wayne yanked on the cable, pulling Orion behind him. "You're not calling the shots here."

As if that wasn't obvious.

Okay, so maybe going at it alone hadn't been the smartest thing to do.

We're a body for a reason. We don't fight alone.

Amos was stubborn, but he was right too. No amount of training or strength was going to help him overpower all these men. He should've listened to his father.

We know it's a dangerous job, but that's why there's a team. It's not a solo gig. And as your family, we're part of your team too.

But what about everything Orion wanted to prove? That he was a worthy son, a grandson Grandpa Jack could be proud of and not ashamed.

The legacy that is most worth achieving is a life surrendered to God. It's not all up to you.

But Orion was used to being on his own. For so long, he'd been the only one there for his mom. He'd had to hold it together and be there for her.

But then again, look at all she'd done for him. Maybe it really hadn't been on his own strength.

And the two of them had had a lot of support over the years from their community and friends.

Okay, Lord, I get it. I've been pretty focused on what I thought You wanted from me instead of surrendering to You and being a part of the team You brought me to. Help me now. And keep Tori safe.

They followed the trail to the chapel and spilled onto the grassy common area, now marred by muddy tracks and a couple ATVs. But the situation was a little different here. Abraham and Amos held a bald man. Three others from the militia were sitting on the ground, surrounded by men from the commune.

Hannah and Mara ran down the steps of the chapel.

And the fire was roaring toward them all.

Amos yelled over to his wife, "Are the other women and children safe?"

Hannah coughed and nodded. "All the women and children are accounted for if Tori is out here with you. But we should all be inside. The smoke—"

Orion scanned the area. A fist-sized lump lodged in his throat. "Where's Tori?"

"I didn't say you could talk," Frank said. "Doyle, are all our people here?"

The man Amos had in hand looked around. "All except Damian."

"Good riddance. That idiot thought this was Tristan. He's the one that sent us on this messed-up chase." Frank kept his gun pointed at Orion.

"Hey, that's my cousin you're talking about." One of the men behind Orion stepped up.

"So you wanna be responsible for his fiasco?" Frank asked him.

The man backed down.

"We need to get inside," Mara said, a worried expression on her face as she looked over the top of the chapel at the flames coming closer.

"I'm not going anywhere until you release my men." Frank practically snarled.

"Release our man and we'll seek shelter together. We don't want any trouble." Amos faced the militiaman. "We have enough room in the basement of the chapel until the fire passes us by."

But Tori.

For a moment, the men faced each other in a silent stare down.

"You're just going to let us walk on out of here when this is done? I don't believe you," Frank said.

Amos didn't back down. "I'm a man of my

word. I don't want to see anyone harmed. If you agree to leave us in peace."

"Fine, but let us go. We'll find our own way out of this fire."

"What about Tori?" Orion yanked his wrists, the thin cable cutting into his skin. But with the woman he loved missing, he didn't much care.

Amos nodded at his men, and they released the militia, who immediately ran for the ATVs.

Orion ran after the one related to Damian. "Where is Tori? Did your cousin—"

"If she's the blonde trainer from the gym, there's no telling what Damian has done. But I'm not waiting around to find out. He's on his own." He swung a leg over behind Vlad on the seat of the four-wheeler, and they peeled out of the commune.

A strong hand on his shoulder stopped Orion from sprinting after them. They disappeared into the smoke.

"Hold on, son." Amos released the locking mechanism on the snare, freeing Orion's wrists.

"I have to find her." His eyes were already watering from the smoke in the air.

"We'll go with you," Abraham said. John, Mara's brother, stood next to him.

"I can't have you risk your lives—"

"You don't have to do this alone, Orion. We can cover more ground together." Amos looked past Orion and over the chapel roof. "Look, the fire is moving south. That's because, together, we worked on that fire line the way you taught us. One man could not have done it. God brought you here for a reason. To help us. And also for us to help you get your wife back."

Orion followed the outline of flames. The line was holding.

And the truth of Amos's words pinched in uncomfortable ways. But he was right. Except for one thing.

"She's not my wife." In that moment, the truth of the matter crystallized. "I'm hopelessly in love with her, but . . . we're not actually married."

But he wanted to explore that possibility in the future. She was fire and light. Passion and adventure.

Life before moving here had been full, but looking back, it seemed dull and stale. She brought a joy he wanted to discover for himself. He needed to find her. Now.

Amos studied him a beat, his eyes narrowed. "She still needs saving, and you still need our help."

But what had Amos said earlier? *Cover more ground.*

Right. Orion needed to dial down the pride and realize they *were* better off working together.

And his team was bigger than the four of them standing here in the middle of the Refuge.

He found the radio. "Price to base. We need help. Tori is missing, possibly kidnapped."

Tucker's voice came through. "What's your location?"

"At the Refuge. The fire is skirting around us, heading south and east. Most likely, if Tori was taken, they'll be following the river north of here."

"We've got the Firehawk chopper in the air with another load of water. We'll have them fly over and scope it out. The rest of the team is on the way to help."

But would they get there in time?

Tori had gotten into smokejumping because it was the most dangerous job she could think of. She wanted to prove to herself that she could face her fears and overcome them. That she wasn't a helpless little girl afraid of the dark. Or a lost, broken teenager so scared to be alone that she found herself in even darker places if it meant she could, for a little bit of time, feel like she belonged.

Yet here she was, very much alone and now blindfolded.

Well, not completely alone. The sound of water and rhythmic splashing meant she was still in the canoe with *him*.

Damian.

Sure, as a client he'd always wanted more attention, a little more handholding than others, but she'd never thought he was this sick.

"It's about time you woke up."

Tori pushed herself up to sitting, ready for a showdown. So her head was a little fuzzy still. She had enough wits to fight. Starting with ripping off the blindfold. "What do you think you're doing? Kidnapping me?"

He glanced back and continued to paddle. "You weren't paying attention. I needed to get you away from that other guy, from your friends. You don't need them."

"For what?"

"To build a new life. Together." He turned in the seat and let the paddle rest on his lap. The current carried them slowly downstream.

"With you? What makes you think—wait. Are you part of the militia? Is that what this is?"

"They were a means to an end. They're busy killing off some fish, testing drones to release toxins, and establishing a new order. But what they're forgetting is our greatest asset: our children."

His straight face and soulless eyes as he spoke gave her goosebumps. "You have kids?" That was a scary thought.

"Not yet." He paused. "But I've found the perfect mother for my children. A woman who's strong. Fit. Beautiful." He lifted his hand to caress her.

She balked, dangerously rocking the canoe. The man was more than sick. He was completely delusional. "What about that girl, the one you were with at the bar?"

"Amber? I told you. She was a friend. She doesn't have the strength needed for this new life. We need to populate, establish a new generation. One that can fight back. Think for themselves. I've watched you for a while now. You're the one. The others can worry about governments and establishments. I'm thinking of the future."

Tori glanced around. Not a thing to use as a weapon or restraint in the vessel. She needed to get away from him and run. It wasn't too far to the shore. She had no idea how long she'd been knocked out for or how far they'd gone. The air was still smoky. The fire was still out there.

"Well, I hate to break it to you, but I'm not part of that future, Damian. I'm not drinking the Kool-Aid, not buying into this new way of life."

He didn't look concerned. Instead, a smile creeped on to his face. "Not yet. But you will."

"Not on your life!" She threw herself to the right but then leaped out the left side of the canoe, into the frigid river water. The shock of it stole her breath, but she didn't care. She kicked her legs and came up for air.

Just get to shore. Get to shore.

"Tori!"

Damian couldn't be far behind her. She didn't dare look back to see. She paddled, fought the current, but kept her head above the surface.

Finally, her feet found purchase. She slogged to shore and ran, crashing through underbrush, weaving around the aspen and spruce.

"You can't deny your destiny!" Damian was right behind her. Gaining.

Her head swam. She stumbled. The drugs must still be in her system. She didn't release the whimper crawling up her throat. She knew what Damian was physically capable of. He could outrun her. He was tenacious in the gym. She would have to fight him or outsmart him.

Eyes peeled for a weapon, Tori zigzagged around a stand of birch. There. A tree limb on the ground. She picked it up, tested its weight. It would do. She spun around to face Damian as he approached.

His usually gelled and slightly spiky hair, now plastered to his head, dripped water into his eyes. Eyes that zeroed in on her with a lethal gleam.

"That wasn't nice, Tori."

"Neither is drugging me. Or kidnapping me. You can't seriously think you're going to win me over this way."

"I knew it would take some time for you to come around, but you'll see. I always get what I want."

Tori lunged and swung the branch, aiming for his knee. He jumped out of the way and grabbed the end of the branch. She wrested it out of his grip and swung again. If she could keep him off guard, she'd have a chance. Her swing caught him in the middle. He fell, but as he did, he swept his leg, knocking her to the ground. She scrambled away, still holding her weapon. He grabbed her by the foot and yanked her back, his arms taking hold of her torso.

No. Way.

She jerked her head back, smacking his nose. His hold loosened and she broke free.

Tightening her grip, once again she swung. The branch smashed into his head. Damian collapsed.

Tori backed away, not taking her eyes off him. Her free hand brushed against the smooth, papery bark of a birch. She grasped it, needing something solid to hold on to. She leaned back against it and tried to catch her breath. She should run. As far away as she could. But she needed a moment. Just a moment.

She fought to bring her heart rate back down.

Damian still didn't move.

Good. Now she could—

A crashing through the underbrush alerted her.

A high-pitched animal sound, almost like a short bark, spiked her pulse once more. Tori turned slowly. There, in a small clearing, stood a baby moose. A very young moose from the looks of it. And it still probably had a hundred pounds on her.

Tori spun. The cow had to be close, and she didn't want to be in the way of a mother and her child.

The calf called again.

This time, Mom answered with a deeper, longer bellow that had the hair on the back of Tori's neck prickling. The cow must be moving in fast. There was nowhere else to go but up. Tori dropped her branch and grabbed the lowest limb on the birch tree. She climbed as high as she could go on the middle tree, the thickest trunk.

The moose reunited in the clearing, right under Tori. And neither seemed eager to move from the spot.

From her height, Tori could see the fire in the distance, flames flying high above the canopy, torching everything in its path. Thankfully, it was on the opposite side of the river. Once the moose left, she could follow the water back to the Refuge. Or she could take the canoe. It was turned upside down, half in the river, the front snagged between two boulders on the shore.

A rustling drew Tori's attention back to Damian. He roused. The moose wandered into the trees again and away from Tori's birch.

This is not the timing I had in mind, Lord.

Damian sat up and spotted her immediately.

"This wasn't how it was supposed to be." He stood and brushed himself off. Blood ran down the side of his face from his temple.

Tori adjusted her grip on the tree trunk as it

swayed. "Damian, look. I am not the woman for you. You want a sweet girl who is—"

"Don't tell me what I want!" He looked around. Felt his pockets. He pulled a lighter out of his wet trail pants. He flicked it, but nothing happened. He grabbed the branch that Tori had hit him with.

"Damian, what are you doing?"

He ran the wheel of the lighter on the bark. "I gave you a chance. I actually appreciated your strength of mind." He rolled the lighter again and again. "But I miscalculated. I should've groomed you more. But you'll learn. You'll die wishing you'd chosen me."

The lighter sparked.

He lit the limb on fire, the birch bark catching quickly. With it, he set fire to the base of the trees surrounding the one Tori was clinging to.

"Are you crazy? Stop! You'll light this whole forest on fire!"

"Goodbye, Tori." He dropped the burning branch and jogged back to the canoe.

"Damian!"

He flipped the canoe over and climbed in.

Thick smoke curled up, choking Tori. She coughed, grabbed her shirt to cover her nose.

The hymn she'd kept hearing at the Refuge ran through her mind.

> *Through many dangers, toils, and snares,*
> *I have already come:*
> *'Tis grace has brought me safe thus far,*
> *And grace will lead me home.*

Here she was in the middle of the danger. Where was grace?

It had been there in the hospital when Orion had stayed by her side. She'd prayed and known God was there. Had she lost Him already?

What was it Orion had said?

He wants you, Victoria.

Wanted.

He is light. And He's not going to leave you or push you away. He's always with you.

Good. Cuz she could use some help.

Lord, I cried out in that hospital bed, and I believe You rescued me then. If what Orion said is true, then You're here too. And I could use another rescue. And . . . thank You for not leaving me alone. Lead me home, to safety.

And though she couldn't explain it, the thought settled deep down to her bones.

No matter what happened, she would be okay.

FIFTEEN

ORION PEERED FROM THE RESCUE helicopter. The S-70 Firehawk with its pilot and two crew members had arrived today from an Oregon base to help the out-of-control wildfire. The timing couldn't be a coincidence.

He's the Good Shepherd.

Strapped in, Orion leaned to see out the other side's windows, but with the smoke and ash blocking his view, it was useless. He hated not being able to see.

"He couldn't have gotten that far," he said into the microphone. Damian, that creep from the gym, must've taken Tori in the chaos of the militia showing up at the commune.

"We're following the river. Won't stop till we find her." The pilot's voice was confident.

The river made the most sense. Amos and Abraham had been the ones to realize one of their canoes was missing. And being the ones who could paddle fastest, since Orion's shoulder was out of commission, they'd launched a canoe and taken off to look for her.

And here Orion sat on his backside, riding around. What would Grandpa Jack think of this failure of a fire season?

I'm sure your mother and your grandfather, if he were alive, would be proud of you, even if you weren't a smokejumper. They'd be proud of you because of the kind of man you are, not because of the rescue work you do.

Tori's words came back to him, choking him up a little.

And what was it his father had said to him?

The legacy that is most worth achieving is a life surrendered to God. It's not all up to you.

But this was Tori's life on the line. Shouldn't he be doing more?

Oh, this trust thing was hard. To surrender and wait rather than relying on his own ability and achievements.

Okay, Lord, this is all up to You. All I can do is sit

here, be along for this ride. I have to trust this rescue. This mission is in Your hands. Please protect her.

"Looks like the fire jumped the river up ahead," the pilot said.

Orion squinted. Below, in the river, Amos and Abraham were in the canoe. And farther upstream, a column of smoke rose from the north side of the river.

"Weird. There's nothing else on fire there. Just one cluster of birch trees." A woman in a rescue jumpsuit sat next to another rescue worker across from Orion. "There's a canoe upriver. Is that her?" She pointed out the window.

Orion searched the water ahead.

The canoe was farther than the one Abraham and Amos paddled. And it only had one occupant. With that build, it couldn't be Tori.

"It's not her. But I think that's Damian. The one who kidnapped her."

What had Damian done with her? Orion fisted his hands around the straps holding him in.

He studied the fire in the trees again. A bright red bandanna waved in the air. Blonde hair blew in the wind.

Orion's heart stopped. Tori! "She's in the trees! The ones on fire! Tell me there's water in this tank."

"No, but it only takes forty-five seconds to fill," the pilot said.

The helicopter lowered until it hovered over the river, the rotor wash spraying the windows. It had to be the longest forty-five seconds in history, but soon the helicopter was back in the air.

Hold on, Tori.

The Firehawk rose and then released the water right on top of the trees. A cloud of steam hid everything for a moment.

Orion couldn't breathe.

"Oscar, you got a basket ready?" the pilot asked the man sitting across from Orion.

"Got it." He stood, harness already strapped, and within seconds, the woman helped guide the drop.

Strapped to the helicopter seat like he was, Orion could only watch. Oscar and the basket descended into the steam and smoke.

Please, Lord, let her be okay. Please.

Wind blew in from the open door. Still no sign of them.

Finally, Oscar's voice came through the comms. "Ready to hoist."

The winch moved, rolling up cable. The rescue worker stood in the doorway, a thick-belted harness around her waist anchoring her as she leaned out.

Coming out of the gray cloud was Tori in a basket, her face covered in ash and blood, but she was very much alive as she coughed. Oscar was right behind her. Together with the other rescue worker, he transferred Tori out of the basket. As soon as she was free, she was in Orion's arms.

"I was so afraid I wasn't ever going to see you . . . that I'd never be able to tell you—" She sobbed, wiping tears and soot from her face.

Even so, she had to be the most beautiful thing God had ever made.

"Tell me what?" Orion removed the helmet he'd been wearing and rested his forehead against hers.

"I love you," her voice croaked.

He drank her in, grateful beyond words to be holding her. "I've loved you from the moment you taught me to dance and every day since then."

She laughed. "Really?"

"You are the bravest, most amazing woman I've ever met. And if I have to, I'll marry you all over again to prove it." He kissed her, pouring all the passion and love he had for this incredible woman into the connection.

As they hovered in the sky somewhere between

heaven and earth, Orion knew. She was the adventure he'd been looking for, and he never wanted it to end.

Tori stared out the window as the Firehawk landed in the middle of the Refuge. The common area still thrived, green and grassy. The garden was full of plants finally starting to take off. But all the land surrounding the community was burnt and black, much of it still smoldering and smoking. The rescue workers helped Tori and Orion out of the helicopter.

Logan, Hammer, and Skye welcomed them with hugs all around.

"How did you guys get here?" Orion asked them.

Logan nodded off to the side of the chapel. "On the ATVs over there. It pays to have a girlfriend with connections."

"Jamie did that?" Tori studied the four-wheelers. They looked sparkling and new.

Logan threw an arm around Orion's shoulder. "You guys risked your lives to help her. She wanted to return the favor."

Gabby broke through the crowd. She hugged Tori tightly. "I'm so glad you're okay."

"Thanks, kiddo. You were a big help fighting that fire."

She practically glowed at the compliment. But then her attention snagged on Logan. "Is he married?" she whispered.

They all laughed.

Skye pulled them aside to where her husband stood. "Rio has been in contact with the Firehawk pilot and the sheriff."

Rio had to speak loudly to be heard above the chopper rotors. "Is the guy who kidnapped you out there?" He sounded much more like the FBI agent he was than the casual guy who hung out with Skye at base camp.

Tori nodded. "Damian Murphy. He lit the tree I climbed on fire and left in a canoe."

"Two of the men from the Refuge here were pursuing him." Orion's arm around her waist steadied her.

"Is Damian part of the militia?" Rio asked.

She nodded. "He at least knows what's going on. He mentioned dead fish and the drone attack. I don't think he's involved at a leadership level, but he has info."

"Good. I'm going to catch a ride with these guys and bring him in. We'll need to have an official statement from you later." Rio shook their hands and then jogged over to the helicopter pilot. Soon the bird was up in the air again.

Children ran out of the chapel to watch the spectacle, awe and wonder in their faces. The rest of the team introduced themselves to the kids. Hammer walked over to Joann and Josiah and asked to hold the baby.

Hannah came and grabbed Tori in a fierce hug. "The Lord bless and keep you, Victoria."

Tears smarted her eyes. "He already has." She grabbed Orion's hand. "In more ways than one."

"I know this lifestyle isn't for everyone, but I hope you both know, you're always welcome here if you ever need a refuge or a home." Hannah's wrinkled face beamed with affection and warmth.

Tori took it all in. Her teammates laughing with the children, the green forest life protected from the fire, and a man—a good man, kind and loving—at her side. Above them all, the sunlight shone, catching the cross at the top of the chapel building and creating a shadow on the lawn where they stood.

She knew who she belonged to now. She didn't need to fear the darkness. And she would never be alone again.

'Tis grace has brought me safe thus far, and grace will lead me home.

THANK YOU

Thank you so much for reading *Burning Escape*. We hope you enjoyed the story. If you did, would you be willing to do us a favor and leave a review? It doesn't have to be long- just a few words to help other readers know what they're getting. (But no spoilers! We don't want to wreck the fun!) Thank you again for reading!

We'd love to hear from you—not only about this story, but about any characters or stories you'd like to read in the future.

Contact us at www.sunrisepublishing.com/contact.

READ ON FOR MORE FROM

CHASING FIRE:
ALASKA

Gear up for the next Chasing Fire: Alaska romantic suspense thriller, *Burning Secrets* by Susan May Warren.

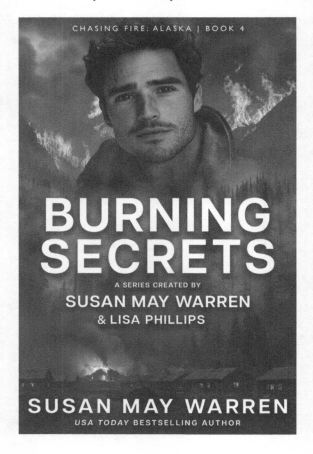

CHASING FIRE: ALASKA | BOOK 4

BURNING SECRETS

A SERIES CREATED BY
SUSAN MAY WARREN
& LISA PHILLIPS

SUSAN MAY WARREN

USA TODAY BESTSELLING AUTHOR

RESCUE. DANGER. DEVOTION. THIS TIME, THEIR HEARTS ARE ON THE LINE.

Wrong place, wrong time…

Wildlife biologist JoJo Butcher isn't just a smokejumper for the Midnight Sun crew—she's also in Alaska to finish up her wolf research…until, oops, she finds herself face-to-face with a wolf with nowhere to go…

And then she's rescued by a hero from the woods. Who exactly is he, and what secrets is he hiding?

He's living a double life…

Undercover FBI informant Michael Crew Sterling hates his life. Buried deep inside a domestic terrorist group, he's in over his head, trying to discover their lethal plans. And then he saves the life of JoJo Butcher, and suddenly she is sunshine to his dark soul…

Until she accidentally walks into nightmare.

Now Crew must keep her alive by proving that she's his girlfriend. And she has to play along, or they'll both be killed. And when they discover what the group is really doing, Crew will have to make a choice that could cost him everything he's sacrificed to save the woman he's falling for.

Book four in the epic Chasing Fire: Alaska series is an edge-of-your seat tale of danger, loyalty, and the power of hope in the darkest night.

ONE

NORMAL PEOPLE, ON THEIR DAY OFF, might go into town, grab a pizza, a chocolate shake, maybe hang out with the other smoke-jumpers.

But apparently, she wasn't normal.

Although, JoJo might have thought to take her tracker ring with her so that when she was mauled and left for dead in the high Alaskan woods, someone might find her carcass and inform her poor mother.

After five years watching her daughter jump out of airplanes into the mouth of the dragon, her worst fears would come true on a bright, sunny day in a clump of wild blueberry bushes.

JoJo held her breath, didn't move as the grizzly,

his feral scent souring the air, snuffled through the thick bushes, hunting for lunch. He'd come up on her like smoke, as if from nowhere, just the redolence of him a hint of trouble as she'd trained her binoculars some forty yards ahead to a secluded burrow near the river.

Please, let the pups still be alive.

The river—just a meandering tributary off the main channel of the Copper River that ran from the lumbering Denali massif—carved out caves and indentations as it cut south through tundra and alpine woods and splashed over rocky cliffs. She would never have located Cleo and her mate, Brutus, if it weren't for the tracking collars the ADF&G had placed on the wolves two years ago.

And she owed wolf researcher and her mentor, Peyton Samson, the thanks for allowing her to observe the mating pair and their pups for her research paper.

Finally put her master's degree to bed.

More snuffing, and the mnemonic from her mother trickled through her head. *If it's black, fight back. If it's brown, lay down.*

As in play dead.

She glanced over, spotted the grizzly scruff of its neck in her peripheral vision, maybe twenty yards away, and slowly lowered herself to the stony earth, pulling her hood up, her body in the fetal position.

Her heartbeat rushed in her ears, nearly deafening.

Breathe. Don't move.

And for some reason, Jade Ransom, her jump boss, entered her head. *Where do you go on your days off? You're always disappearing.*

Yeah, maybe she shouldn't be quite so private. It wasn't like she was breaking any laws. She just preferred the quiet, the aloneness. No one to get in her way.

No one to break her heart. The breath of the Alaska air, just her and the wilderness.

Maybe she was like her father in that way. She hoped so.

Sticks broke, more rustling. Snuffing.

Her hand trekked down her leg to her bear spray in her thigh holster. Who knew if it might actually repel the grizzly? Better to hide. But should the animal—

Barking. Then a growl and more barking, and she wanted to push herself up, to see if—

Yes, it sounded like Brutus. Maybe protecting his den.

Weird that Cleo wasn't with him, but JoJo

hadn't seen the pups, so maybe Cleo was out hunting. Still, alone? That didn't feel right.

Although, recently, a lot didn't feel right. Like her team's recent run-in with some crazy Alaskan militia group who'd tried to kill them.

And never mind the *plane crash* that they'd narrowly escaped. Then, while they'd hiked back to civilization, her other team members had been chased down, met a rogue cult, found dead salmon in a river, found a homesteader lady in the woods who'd been drugged, and one of the team had been *kidnapped*.

She hadn't been sad they'd left without her on that spur-of-the-moment trip. Still, it felt like the entire world had gone crazy up here in the land of the never-ending sun.

The grizzly growled, turning, breaking branches, trampling the bushes.

She pushed herself up. All around her on the hillside, blueberry bushes poked up around boulders. The hill pitched down to a ten-foot drop into a rocky riverbed and its glistening river in the valley below.

Brutus paced on a large flat-topped rock, his fur ruffed, barking, foam at his mouth. The grizzly lumbered nearby, nearly ignoring him as he foraged.

Where was his pack? She lifted her glasses, scanned the area. Brutus and Cleo had returned to the den they'd used last year. The pack usually congregated in and around the craggy shoreline. This year, however, they seemed more scattered, the pack thinner.

He wouldn't take on a bear without the pack. Not unless . . .

He hadn't gotten ousted as alpha, had he? She searched his body for wounds, evidence of a fight.

Brutus rushed at the bear, who turned, swatted. Brutus jerked away, snarling, barking.

The bear landed on all fours, growled, and then shook his head side to side. Agitated. Nervous.

Watch out, Brutus. The grizzly huffed, stomped, but Brutus stood his ground, snapping, growling, barking.

She tucked away her bear spray, picked up her phone. Snapped a picture.

And then, just like that, the bear moved off, turning, lumbering away.

Brutus climbed the flat stone, barking after it. Still growling.

She stood, took another picture of the wolf, deep-gray hair along its body, white tufted hair between his legs and along his snout, dark black eyes, a bushy light-gray tail, a ring of black at the end.

A beautiful alpha male. And maybe he'd just saved her life.

And this, right here, was why she'd come to Alaska. Sure, she'd joined the Midnight Sun fire crew, but that had simply landed her on the map in the right place. Given her a reason to show up at the Forest Service office in search of Professor Samson, who'd guest taught for a week at Montana State University in Bozeman.

Right then, JoJo had known what she wanted to do with her life.

Study these animals, discover what made them fierce and brave and enabled them to thrive in the harsh Alaskan frontier.

Maybe figure out how to do the same.

Brutus turned and looked at her, straight on. The breeze picked up, rustled the brush, combed through his hair.

He didn't seem displaced from leadership.

And then he growled. A low, lethal warning.

Oh. She pocketed her phone. Kept eye contact. "No need for that, Brute." *Get bigger.* She spotted a rock, climbed on it. Raised her arms.

His growl deepened, and he lowered his head.

"I'm not the bad guy!" She clapped her hands.

"Go away!" She grabbed her whistle, blew it, piercing, bright, shrill.

He raised his lips in a snarl.

What was his deal? She'd gotten too close once, and he'd emerged from the den, but she'd simply backed away, and he'd let her go.

"I'm not going to hurt your pups, Brute." She clapped her hands, then unzipped her jacket and held it open. "Go away!"

He took a step toward her, and she reached for her bear spray. "Don't make me use this—"

The wolf launched at her.

She screamed, stumbled back, slipped and slammed into the bramble, bounced off, hit the rocky edge with her hip.

Pain exploded through her body, but she rolled, found the spray. Screamed.

Brutus appeared above her, snarling, barking, nipping.

She deployed the spray as Brutus leaped at her. The spray burned him in the face, and he yelped.

She scrambled for footing. Stood.

He shook off the chemicals and rounded on her, furious.

"Brutus—" She scrambled back. "Don't—"

She sprayed again—nothing. Empty. She took

another step back, threw the can at him, and reached for her gun.

Shoulder holster, and she hated to go for the .44, but she didn't want to be torn limb from limb either. She held it out, took off the safety. "Please, go!" She shouted it, hoping the noise might deter him.

He didn't look right. Pacing, his eyes glossy, foam at his mouth—rabies?

She took another step back and rocks fell. She glanced back—

Brutus launched at her.

She turned, squeezed off a shot, and the recoil jerked her back.

Yelping, she took her eyes off Brutus as she windmilled her arms for purchase, but the momentum yanked her back, and she stumbled into air, the cliff dropping from behind her—

Falling.

She screamed and landed with a hard, brutal *whuff*, ten feet below, her breath jerking out of her body.

Writhing for air, her bones shuddering, everything inside her on fire.

A growl above her, and as she fought to breathe, Brutus appeared over her on the rock above.

She got her hands up just as he leaped.

Breathe! She rolled, waiting for him to land, but a shot broke the air.

Crisp and echoing across the mountainscape.

Brutus dropped next to her on the rocky ground, gone.

She lay breathing, over and over, shaking.

Brutus's glassy eyes stared at her, the life winked out, blood puddling the ground under him.

And all she could do was curl into a ball, hands over her head, and weep.

Please, let him not have killed her.

Crew lowered his Winchester, his body shaking. Picked up his monocular. She lay on the ground, unmoving, the wolf next to her.

He wasn't the best shot, and frankly, he'd end up back in jail if anyone found him in possession of a gun.

But from his vantage point, some four hundred yards away atop a nearby rise that overlooked the Copper River spring, it clearly looked like the wolf had intended on having the woman for dinner.

He'd had no choice—the story of his life, the conundrum driving every decision for the past few weeks since the sister of his cohort Tristan had stumbled onto the Sons of Revolution base camp.

And then the world had just exploded. Literally. The camp had gone up in a ball of fire while Tristan and Jamie had escaped. And then he'd watched a plane of smokejumpers go down, and that had sat in his gut like ash until he'd found out no one had died.

Still, he hated this job.

"Crew—you still there?" The voice crackled in his earpiece, and he jerked, tearing his gaze off the downed woman.

Rio, on the other end of the sketchy transmission. And who knew how much his handler had heard of his report?

"Was that a gunshot? You okay?"

"Not me. Long story—" The phone line cut out, crackled. "Rio?"

Sheesh, the call cut off. Perfect. He worked out his earbud and pocketed it as he strode toward the four-wheeler. Wouldn't be long before Viper and Jer started asking about him, expecting him back from his perimeter sweep.

But he couldn't leave her down there.

From here, the rise fell in a not-so-gentle slope down to the valley floor, but he'd trekked up a deer trail on the backside of the hill, so maybe he could find a way down.

He raced the four-wheeler back to the trail, ducking against bramble and low-hanging, shaggy arms of pine and aspen trees. Emerging onto the valley floor, he turned and gunned the four-wheeler over mossy rocks, crushing magenta fireweed and tall blue lupine and violet wild irises, so much beauty in a brutal land.

The woman wore a blue jacket, hiking boots, and lay still, curled in a ball next to the wolf.

But his heart nearly stopped when she lifted her head. Sat up, staring hard at him.

Pretty. Brown hair, long and in a braid, wide hazel-green eyes, long lashes, a sweetheart face, and it hit him that he'd maybe seen her before.

Maybe around Copper Mountain, one of the many tourists.

He braked.

She lifted a gun.

What? He raised his arms. "Don't shoot."

Her grip shook, and tears glazed her eyes. Had she been crying? "Stay back!"

He eased off the four-wheeler. "Calm down—"

"Calm down? Did you shoot Brutus?"

Who? "Are you hurt?"

She stared at him, her hand still shaking, wiped the other hand across her cheek.

"So maybe put the gun down." He took a step toward her.

"Stay. Back!"

He stopped. Glanced at the mound of fur at her feet. "Listen. I'm sorry about the wolf. I thought he was going to attack you."

She drew in a breath, glanced at the wolf, nodded. "I don't know—he was acting . . . it's not normal."

Not—"What, you two have a long-standing friendship?"

Oops. He'd been kidding, but her gaze snapped up to his.

"Yes, as a matter of fact. I've been studying Brutus and his mate, Cleo, for the past month, watching their cubs, documenting their behavior. And yeah, Brutus has seen me before, but he's never attacked me." Her gun had lowered, her voice breaking. "Something was wrong."

His gaze stayed on the gun. "What kind of wrong?"

"He seemed unhinged, unafraid of me."

"Was he protecting his young?"

She had crouched beside the wolf, lifting his eyelids. "Yes. I don't know. Maybe."

He took another step toward her, the ground crunching beneath his hiking boot.

She looked up. "Stay."

He raised his hands again. "I'm not going to hurt you."

Her eyes narrowed and then glanced at the four-wheeler behind him, and something flashed in her eyes. Fear?

It occurred to him then how he looked—camo jacket, filthy hat over his dark hair, scruffy beard, canvas pants, a .308 Winchester strapped to his machine. The unofficial uniform of a Son of Revolution, and wasn't that nice?

Whatever respite he'd found on top of the hill, away from the darkness, settled right back into his soul, a deep ash that stained everything.

His voice softened. "I was just out checking traps."

Her mouth tightened. "And now I know you're lying, because there is no trapping season open in Alaska right now."

Oh.

Shoot.

He sighed, ran a hand across his chin. "Fine. I'm not out trapping. But I promise I mean you no harm."

"You shot at me!"

"I shot at the wolf. Trying to *kill you*."

She considered him a moment, then shoved her Magnum into her shoulder holster. "Fine. Prove it. Help me get Brutus on your four-wheeler and back to my truck."

He raised an eyebrow. "What?"

She'd started hiking toward the cliff, up the hill from where she'd fallen. "I need to get him to Copper Mountain so we can do an autopsy."

"I think I know how he died." He looked at the wolf. His shot had landed in his body—rib cage—left a bloody through-and-through. Blood caked his fur, puddled the ground, and an odor lifted. Gross.

"Don't be a jerk," she said, now from atop the cliff. She held a backpack. "Listen—okay, yes, he was . . ."

"Attacking you?"

"Acting deranged. Maybe rabies, so yes, thank you." She turned and headed back down the hill.

He crouched. The animal had blood in its teeth, foam at its lips. A feral odor lifted from its body.

Her boots crunched up to him. "Do you have a tarp or anything?"

He stood up. She wasn't tall—maybe five inches shorter than him—but she owned a presence about her that suggested she fancied herself in charge. Blood prickled along a scrape on her jaw. "You sure you're okay? That's not a short fall." He indicated the cliff. "Maybe you need to get checked out."

"I've had harder falls, believe me. Tarp?"

His eyes narrowed a moment, then he headed over to the four-wheeler and opened up the seat. Wire, ammo, knife, the radio to the compound—turned off—a fire-starting kit, a rope, and there, grimy and wadded on the bottom, an orange rain poncho. He pulled it out. Shook it open. "This could work."

"Thanks, MacGyver." She took it. "Help me roll this guy into it."

"Tell me again why we're bringing this show-and-tell to Copper Mountain?"

She'd crouched and spread the poncho out on the ground beside the wolf. He helped her and then took the animal's front legs as she took the back, and they rolled it onto the plastic.

"There's some rope too." He went to retrieve the rope and knife.

"I think he might have ingested something—a hallucinogenic or maybe eaten some poison." She wrapped the animal in the poncho, held the poncho shut as he secured it with the rope, making a sort of bundle.

Her words were a punch. Hallucinogenic? Oh no . . . He stared at the wolf, the darkness seeping into his bones, his breath. And then her other word hit him. *Ingested.* "As in he ate something?"

"Maybe. Take that end. Let's lift him."

He grabbed the animal and helped her lift him onto the back of the four-wheeler. Secured him with a couple bungie ropes, the math of her words freezing him through.

The food supply.

Oh no. But it made sense—

She'd stepped away from the four-wheeler, pulled out a monocular, and now scanned the riverbed.

"What are you looking for?"

"The pups. And his alpha female, Cleo." She sighed, turned. "You haven't seen anything . . . like dead salmon in the river, have you?"

He raised an eyebrow. "Why?"

And the answer, of course, was yes. Oh no, *yes.* He wanted to hit something.

"Just . . . nothing." She frowned. Eyed his four-wheeler again, then looked at him, her jaw tight. And he didn't know why, but he had the strangest urge to raise his hands again.

Silence thrummed between them, back-dropped by the river rushing by, the hush lifting into the breeze.

"Who are you again?" she asked.

And for a second, he was back on the cliff, twenty minutes before he'd taken the shot, waiting for Rio to text him. Staring at the blue sky, the clouds congregating at the peak of the Denali massif. Surveying the vast green of the aspen and Sitka spruce, the craggy gray of the jutting mountains, the wildflower beauty of the valley. Even smelling the crisp, boreal-scented wind and hearing his own voice.

Lord, I need light. I need hope. I need answers. I need out.

And maybe that's why he looked at her, took a breath, and said the first true thing he'd said in over a year. "My name is Michael Crew Sterling. And I promise you, I'm one of the good guys." He stuck out his hand. "You can call me Crew."

She considered him a moment. A long, fragile moment where his hand sort of hung in the wind.

Then she sighed and took it. "I'm going to choose to trust you, Crew. Joann Butcher. My friends call me JoJo."

"Are we friends, then?"

Her mouth pinched. "As long as you don't try and kill me."

His mouth quirked. "Not real high standards, then. I think I have a real chance here."

She frowned, and then just like that, laughed. It emerged light and sweet and maybe a little short, but with it, light simply poured into his soul, swept out his breath.

He stared at her, nearly clutched his chest.

Yes, he wanted out, and now.

"Let's get going so I can get back and figure out if his pups are in trouble."

Oh.

He climbed onto the four-wheeler. Moved his foot so she could climb up behind him, her legs around his, her body against his back.

"Hang on," he said. "It's bumpy."

"I'm not going anywhere," she said, and gripped the side handles on the seat.

And as he pulled out across the bumpy terrain, all he could think was . . . I hope not.

AKNOWLEDGEMENTS

As with every book I'm able to write, the acknowledgements are never adequate enough thanks for the many who helped make it this far. To my mentors and editors, fellow writers and friends, and especially my family, I am grateful for all you do and how you've shown up for me, especially in this valley season. From the depths of my heart I say, "Thank you!"

After growing up on both the east and west coasts, **Michelle Sass Aleckson** now lives the country life in central Minnesota with her own hero and their four kids. She loves rocking out to 80's music on a Saturday night, playing Balderdash with the fam, and getting lost in good stories. Especially stories that shine grace. And if you're wondering, yes, Sass is her maiden name.

Visit her at www.michellealeckson.com

CHASING FIRE:
ALASKA

Dive into an epic series created by

SUSAN MAY WARREN
and LISA PHILLIPS

DIVE INTO AN EPIC JOURNEY IN BOOK ONE OF
CHASING FIRE: MONTANA

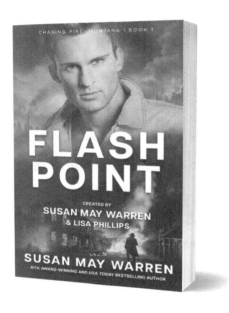

*The Hollywood heartthrob and
the firefighter with a secret...*

What could go wrong?

WE THINK YOU'LL ALSO LOVE...

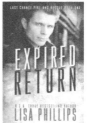

Fire Department liaison Allen Frees may have put his life back together, but getting the truck crew and engine squad to succeed might be his toughest job yet. When a child is nearly kidnapped, Allen steps in to help Pepper Miller keep her niece safe. The one thing he couldn't fix was the love he lost, but he isn't going to let Pepper walk away this time.

Expired Return by Lisa Phillips

Stunt double Vienna Foxcroft's stunt team are the only ones she trusts. Then in walks Sergeant Crew Gatlin and his tough-as-nails military dog, Havoc. When an attack on a film set sends them fleeing into the streets of Turkey, Vienna must face the demons of her past or be devoured by them. And Crew and Havoc will be tested like never before.

Havoc by Ronie Kendig

When an attempt is made on Grey Parker's life and dead bodies begin piling up, suddenly bodyguard Christina Sherman is tasked with keeping both a soldier and his dog safe... and with them, the secrets that could stop a terrorist attack.

Driving Force by Lynette Eason and Kate Angelo

sunrise
PUBLISHING

**WHERE EVERY STORY IS A FRIEND,
AND EVERY CHAPTER IS A NEW JOURNEY...**

Subscribe to our newsletter for a free book, the latest news, weekly giveaways, exclusive author interviews, and more!

follow us on social media!

Made in United States
Cleveland, OH
24 June 2025

17957155R00173